Praise for Robin Lee Hatcher

"Nobody addresses modern women's issues better than Robin Lee Hatcher. Thank you, Robin Lee, for writing about pain and struggle and, therefore, the unfathomable grace of a living, caring, Holy God. Thank you for offering hope and redemption on every page."
—Lisa Samson, author of
The Passion of Mary-Margaret

"Hatcher knows what the reader wants and always delivers."
—*RT Book Reviews* on *Fit to Be Tied*

"Hatcher's pleasingly smooth prose makes this novel a delight."
—*Publishers Weekly* on *The Victory Club*

"Romantic fare perfect for curling up in front of the fireplace with a cup of hot chocolate."
—*Library Journal* on *Hearts Evergreen*

"Hatcher knows what the reader wants and always delivers."
—*RT Book Reviews* on *Fit to Be Tied*

ROBIN LEE HATCHER

is a winner of the Christy Award for Excellence in Christian Fiction, two RITA® Awards, two *RT Book Reviews* Career Achievement Awards, and the Romance Writers of America Lifetime Achievement Award. She is the author of more than seventy novels and lives in Idaho.

Bundle of Joy
Robin Lee Hatcher

Refreshed version of DADDY CLAUS,
revised by the author

HARLEQUIN® LOVE INSPIRED®

Recycling programs for this product may not exist in your area.

™ LOVE INSPIRED BOOKS

ISBN-13: 978-0-373-78796-8

BUNDLE OF JOY

Copyright © 1999 as DADDY CLAUS by Robin Lee Hatcher

Copyright © 2008 as BUNDLE OF JOY by Robin Lee Hatcher

www.Harlequin.com

Printed in U.S.A.

Don't you see that children are God's best gift?
  the fruit of the womb his generous legacy?
    Like a warrior's fistful of arrows
    are the children of a vigorous youth.
    Oh, how blessed are you parents,
    with your quivers full of children!
Your enemies don't stand a chance against you;
  you'll sweep them right off your doorstep.
              —*Psalms* 127:3–5

Prologue

Alicia: I don't know what I'll do.

Joe: May I make a suggestion? You could tell your grandfather the truth.

Alicia: I can't do that. It would break his heart. I lied in the first place to protect him. He was so sick. No one thought he would survive his heart attack. And when he did, I never *dreamed* the doctor would allow him to travel. I thought I would have more time.

Joe: "Oh, what a tangled web we weave, when first we practice to deceive!"

Alicia: Very funny.

Joe: Sorry.

Joe: :-\

Joe: Thought Sir Walter Scott had a good point.

Alicia: Not in this circumstance. Grandpa's from the old school. There's never been a divorce in the Harris family. And he warned me not to be hasty. If he finds out the truth, he'll worry about me. That's not good for his heart. It might kill him. Oh, how did I get myself into this mess?

Joe: What you need is rent-a-husband.

Joe: ;-)

Alicia: Ha! You applying for the position, Joe?

Joe: Six weeks pretending to be your husband? Sounds like pretty gruesome work to me.

Alicia: So much for the rent-a-husband idea. I think I need a good cry. Ought to last about a week.

Joe: Hey! Don't cry. It wouldn't be *that* gruesome. As I recall, you were a pretty cute ten-year-old. I suppose I could stomach it if I had to.

---Joe: Alicia?

---Joe: Alicia? Are you there?

---Joe: Hello?

Alicia: I'm here. I was just thinking about what you said. Maybe this could work.

Joe: What could work?

Alicia: You pretending to be my husband for a few weeks. Just while Grandpa is here. Maybe it's the perfect solution. You want to move back to Idaho, and you'll need to find a position. That takes time, especially during the holidays. This would give you somewhere to stay. I've got extra bedrooms. By the new year, you'd be employed and have a place of your own.

Joe: I hope you're not serious.

Alicia: But I *am* serious. Not just serious. Desperate!

---Alicia: Joe?

Joe: My turn to think.

Alicia: Will you do it?

---Alicia: Joe?

Joe: Tell you what. I'm flying up next week anyway. We'll meet and talk while I'm in town. Then if you still want to go through with this crazy idea of yours, I'll consider it. But no promises.

Alicia: It was *your* crazy idea.

Joe: I know. But I was kidding.

Chapter One

The streets of downtown Boise were busy on this second Saturday in November. People walked briskly along the sidewalks, their coat collars turned up and their heads leaning into the wind as they hurried from store to store. Shops and restaurants were crowded. A good sign for retailers, since the Christmas shopping season hadn't begun in earnest.

Alicia Harris sat at a table in Espresso Heaven, a coffee shop on Main Street, waiting anxiously for someone who looked like Joe Palermo—thirty-six years old, six foot two, black hair, brown eyes—to walk through the door. It wasn't much of a description, but it was all he'd given her. It didn't matter. She was certain she would recognize him, even after all these years.

No, it wasn't the description—or lack thereof—that made her anxious. It was wondering whether or not he would agree to her outlandish suggestion. If he didn't…

"Care for some coffee while you wait?" the waitress asked, drawing Alicia's gaze from the street scene.

"No, thanks. But I would like some herbal tea, if you have any."

"Sure thing. Whole selection. Be right back."

Alicia laid a hand on her extended abdomen. "Maybe this *is* a crazy idea, Humphrey." Humphrey was her pet name for her unborn child. "He *could* be an ax murderer."

Joe had suggested that possibility last night when they'd spoken by phone. He'd called from the motel near the airport shortly after checking in.

"You're taking quite a risk, Alicia," he'd said. "You don't know much about me really. Just old memories and some instant messaging. I could be criminally insane. I could be an ax murderer."

She didn't believe he was dangerous. She'd known the entire Palermo family when she was a girl, had made mud pies in the backyard with Joe's younger sister, Belinda. In fact, she'd had a major crush on "Joey" when she was ten and he was seventeen. But the Palermos had moved to California before she could grow up and make him notice her.

No, Joe was no ax murderer. There were plenty of things she didn't know about him, nineteen years later, but she was certain the boy who used to fix her bicycle chains and search for her missing cat was no monster.

A blast of cold air signaled the opening of the coffee shop's door. Alicia glanced up...and stopped breathing.

She was over seven months pregnant and already as big as a barn. She hadn't had a good hair day in at least fifteen weeks. Before leaving the house, she'd hidden the mess under a red-and-black *Cat-in-the-Hat*-type knitted cap. It probably didn't look much better than her hair. To top it all off, three pimples had appeared on her forehead this morning and now glowed as bright and red as Rudolph's nose.

And then there was Joe Palermo.

How did an Adonis at seventeen become even more handsome nearly two decades later? Shouldn't he have wrinkles or a receding hairline or a middle-age paunch or something?

He found her with his eyes, and he smiled.

Good grief! They could light the Capitol Christmas tree with that smile.

She swallowed hard, then smiled in return, watching as he made his way toward her.

Get a grip, Alicia. It's only Joe, and he's just here to consider doing you a favor. He's off-limits.

He stopped on the opposite side of the table. "You must be Alicia." His gaze dropped to her abdomen. "Although you look a little different from the last time I saw you." He glanced up. "You're taller, right?"

"Right." She chuckled nervously.

"It's good to see you again, Alicia."

"You, too, Joe."

He pulled out the chair and slid onto the seat. The waitress appeared before he had time to remove his coat.

"Can I get you something?" she asked, sounding breathless.

"Large coffee. Black. Thanks."

"No frills," Alicia said as the waitress hurried away.

He smiled again. "No frills."

Now she could see she'd been wrong. He *did* have a few wrinkles. Tiny smile lines around his eyes and the corners of his mouth. And mighty attractive they were, too.

Oh, her wacky pregnancy hormones were doing a major number on her. She hadn't given a man the time of day since Grant walked out three weeks after their wedding. She wasn't going to start now. Playing the fool once per decade was her limit.

"Popular place," Joe said, intruding on her thoughts.

"Yes. I usually come about nine in the morning, before I open my store. It's a little more quiet in here then. The eight-to-fivers have come and gone, and I can sit in the corner and sip my tea while reading the paper."

The waitress arrived with Joe's coffee.

"Thanks." He flashed the young woman one of

his million-watt smiles. Then he looked at Alicia, giving the waitress no excuse to linger. "Okay, let's talk about why I'm here."

"No-nonsense. Is that the attorney in you?"

"I guess so."

She sat a little straighter, drew a deep breath and let it out. "Joe, I know this is a huge favor to ask of anyone. Especially since you haven't seen me in years. If there was someone else I could ask…" She sighed. "But there isn't."

"Are you sure this is the best way? I remember your grandfather as the sort of man who would forgive your faults and lend a helping hand when needed. I think he could handle the truth, whatever it is."

"If you'd seen him in the hospital, you'd understand. We came so close to losing him. If he knew I was about to become a single mom, he would worry about me. Worry is the last thing he needs right now."

A frown drew Joe's black eyebrows together. "Proverbs says that truth stands the test of time and lies are soon exposed. I'm thinking that's good advice."

"Is it so terrible to want to protect someone you love?"

"No," he answered softly. "It isn't terrible. Misguided, maybe, but not terrible."

Alicia looked out the window at the scurrying Saturday shoppers. "I never meant for things to get out of hand. I never meant to tell even the first lie. It just sort of…*happened*. It's a long, stupid story."

Joe had come to the café to tell Alicia he couldn't agree to this charade, not even for an old childhood friend. He wasn't a great actor in the best of circumstances. He feared that pretending to be someone's husband—considering his low opinion of wedded bliss—would be beyond his meager capabilities. Besides, he had this troublesome feeling that God would prefer honesty.

But when he opened his mouth to tell her he couldn't do it, out came different words. "Tell me a little more—" he motioned toward her stomach "—about what happened. You haven't gone into detail when we've had our chat sessions."

Still staring toward the window, she released a deep sigh. "It's bad enough my friends and employees know."

"*I'm* your friend, Alicia. You can tell me."

That drew her gaze back to him.

"Hormones," she whispered with a pitiful wave of her hand toward her tear-filled eyes. Then she grabbed her purse, opened it and withdrew a packet of tissues. "Sorry."

"No problem." He sipped his coffee.

After a lengthy silence, she began speaking in a low voice, so low Joe had to lean forward in order to hear her.

"I met Grant Reeves last March at a party. He was an acquaintance of one of my employees and was in town for a few weeks. He was from Reno where he worked as a carpenter. Grant was charming and charismatic. He had a way about him that made all the women take notice. But it was me he paid special attention to that night. And every night after that, too. He wined and dined me, showered me with flowers and gifts. It was all new to me, and I fell hard. He asked me to marry him two weeks later. He wanted to get married right away."

Joe whistled softly, which drew a wry look and a nod from Alicia.

"I called Grandpa Roger. He's the only family I have left since my parents died. I wanted him to be happy for me." As she spoke, she lowered her gaze to the napkin in her hand and began shredding its edges. "But he wasn't. In fact, it brought out the pastor in him." A brief smile curved her mouth, then vanished. "He reminded me that marriage is a holy estate and not to be entered into lightly. He asked questions about Grant's character and wanted to know if he was a Christian. Questions I couldn't answer because I didn't know. Because I hadn't asked them myself."

Joe saw the glitter of tears in her eyes and felt a tug in his heart.

"I got angry and said some very unkind things to Grandpa. And I didn't listen to his words of caution, either. Grant and I were married four days later."

Marry in haste and repent at leisure. Whoever

said that knew what he was talking about. But Joe would have shortened it to: Marry and repent. Period.

"I knew it was a mistake almost from the first day," she continued, "but I wouldn't admit it. My pride was involved. I told myself things would improve. We just had to get used to living together, to each other's idiosyncrasies. I tried not to complain that he spent too much money and that he came home late so often."

Alicia fell silent. Her unshed tears swam before her blue-green eyes. She looked fragile and vulnerable.

All of Joe's protective instincts flared to life. But those instincts weren't good ones, he reminded himself. Better to ignore them.

He took a sip of his lukewarm coffee.

"I found Grant with another woman three weeks after we were married. He seemed surprised I was upset by it. Apparently we had very different ideas of what marriage meant."

"Apparently."

She took a quick breath and let it out. "We got a divorce in Nevada. It only took a few weeks, since Grant was still a resident. It was all relatively painless and civilized. I was relieved I hadn't told Grandpa I'd gotten married." She sighed again.

Joe wondered if she realized how often she did that. The deep breath and audible sigh. The rise and fall of her shoulders. The worrying of her lower lip between her teeth.

"And then I discovered I was pregnant."

"Did you tell Grant?"

"Yes. He said I'd have to prove it was his and accused me of marrying him for child support." She released a self-deprecating laugh. "*This* after he nearly cleaned out my savings account in three weeks' time."

If Grant Reeves had lived within a hundred miles of this coffee shop, Joe would have sought him out and taught that charming, charismatic ne'er-do-well a thing or two.

"I had him sign something where he gave up all of his parental rights. He didn't even hesitate." She sat a little straighter, a spark of determination in her eyes that hadn't been there a moment before. "I don't need anyone to take care of me and the baby. I have my store, and it's doing well. I can support us when the time comes without any help from him or anyone else."

He wondered if she was as independent as she sounded. "Why didn't you tell your grandfather the truth after you discovered you were pregnant?"

"I was going to. I was waiting for the right moment. A time when the truth wouldn't make me look like an idiot."

"You're not an idiot." Misguided, maybe, but not an idiot.

"No. But I felt like one. Anyway, I knew I couldn't keep putting things off. I mean, he was going to know *something* when I went to Arizona for a visit and had a baby with me." She gave him a wry smile. "Grandpa isn't senile."

Joe returned the look.

"He had his heart attack before I could tell him." Her expression sobered. "I rushed down to Arizona to be with him. No one thought he was going to live. Not his doctors. Not his friends. No one. I couldn't very well tell him then."

"And he didn't *notice* you were pregnant?" He couldn't keep the skeptical note out of his voice.

"He was too sick to notice. I was careful how I dressed. Besides, I wasn't very big at the time." She glanced down. "Not like now." She placed both of her hands on her abdomen. "And Humphrey's still got two months to grow."

"Humphrey?"

"That's what I call him. Or her."

"You don't know the sex?"

"I didn't want to. I'd rather be surprised."

He could have told her she sounded as old-fashioned as she thought her grandfather was.

She raised her eyes again. "So…here I am. I didn't tell Grandpa Roger I was married, let alone divorced, because I didn't want him to be disappointed in me. I can't tell him I'm pregnant and alone, because I don't want to worry him and put stress on his weak heart. And now he's coming for an extended holiday visit, and I need a husband. Just for pretend. Just for the holidays."

Joe gave his head a slow shake. "I don't see how

this could work. Your grandfather will be staying with you. Right? Won't he think it odd if your husband doesn't share your bedroom? And I'm guessing sharing your bedroom wasn't part of the pretense you have planned."

Embarrassment rose in her cheeks like a fire. "No, of course not. You won't stay in my room. But I know how to get around it. My room has a door that leads onto the back porch and so does the nursery, which is the room next to mine. That's where you'll sleep at night. When it's time for you to appear, you can go onto the porch, enter through the porch door, and then come out of my bedroom."

He should turn her down. He should tell her how crazy this harebrained scheme sounded. It wasn't as though he owed her a favor. Her family had been good to him, but still—

"It's only for five and a half weeks." Her voice dropped to a whisper. "Please, Joe. There isn't anyone else I can ask."

He must have lost his mind.

"Okay, Alicia. I'll do it."

Chapter Two

Eight days later, at ten minutes after three on a Sunday afternoon, Joe steered his vehicle off the freeway. Every spare inch of the SUV was packed with his possessions. What he hadn't been able to bring with him from California would be shipped later, after he got a place of his own. For now, it was in storage.

He pulled into the parking lot of a convenience store, then reached for his cell phone, flipped it open and dialed Alicia's number. She answered on the third ring.

"It's Joe," he said after her greeting. "I'm in Meridian. Care to give me directions to your place again?"

She did so.

"Sounds easy enough. I ought to be there in about ten, fifteen minutes. If I get lost, I'll call again."

"I'll be watching for you."

"See you soon." He flipped the phone closed.

Undeniably, certifiably insane.

During the past eight days, he'd analyzed why he agreed to her scheme and had come up with a number of answers: She was an old childhood friend. He would be looking for employment in Idaho and so would have time on his hands until he was hired. Her grandfather was a nice guy, and Joe wouldn't want to see anything happen to him because of worry or stress over Alicia.

But the answer he always returned to was this: She was cute. Even big with child and wearing a ridiculous red-and-black hat, she was cute. Not a very good reason to pretend to be her husband for the next five or six weeks.

Yes, he was certifiably nuts.

With a shake of his head, he pulled out of the parking lot and drove south.

The farmland that had once surrounded tiny Meridian, Idaho had been consumed by urban sprawl. Joe had grown used to that in Southern California, but he hadn't expected it here. Not this much.

He took a couple of wrong turns, but eventually he found the big old farmhouse with its screened front porch and half a dozen sixty-foot-tall trees standing like naked sentinels on all sides. Despite its age, the house looked well cared for.

He turned his vehicle into the drive and shut off the engine.

Yeah, he must be crazy.

Taking a deep breath, he opened the car door and stepped out. About the same time, the screen door to the porch screeched a warning, and Alicia came into view. She smiled, waving a greeting with her right hand. He waved back, then grabbed his duffel bag off the car seat and headed toward the house.

"You found me," she said.

Her short-cropped light brown hair looked as if she'd raked her fingers through it moments before; it stuck out in all directions. She wore an oversize sweater that had lost whatever shape it once had, baggy gray sweatpants, and fuzzy pink bunny slippers, complete with floppy ears.

Cute.

"I found you," he replied.

"Come in." She held the door open wider. "I was about to have some herbal tea. Or I've got orange soda and root beer in the fridge, if you prefer, or I can make coffee."

"Tea's fine, but I prefer the regular stuff if you've got it."

"I've got it."

He followed her through a large living area with hardwood floors and an eclectic collection of furniture, including an upright piano and a bronze sculpture of a horse and rider that was reminiscent of a Remington.

The kitchen had the same high ceiling as the living room, but it was cheerier due to large windows framed by lacy curtains instead of heavy brocade drapes, and yellow paint on the walls and cabinets instead of dark paneling and wallpaper. The kitchen was filled with homey little touches, the likes of which Joe hadn't seen since he'd watched *Happy Days* as a kid.

Alicia motioned toward a Formica and chrome table against the far wall. "Have a seat." Then she turned to the stove, lifted a copper teakettle from the back burner and filled two mugs with steaming water.

"How long have you lived here?" Joe settled onto one of the vinyl-upholstered chairs.

"Since the summer after I graduated from high school."

"You were able to *buy* a house when you were eighteen?"

She smiled. "Of course not. It was my grandparents'. When Grandpa Roger retired and they relocated to Arizona, they gave this place to me. I had about eight roommates living with me during my college years. It helped pay the power bill." She set his mug on the table, then sat on the chair opposite him.

"You never wanted to leave Idaho?" he asked.

"What for? Everything I want is here."

"Guess I can't argue with that or I wouldn't be moving back myself." He lifted his mug and took a sip.

That was the precise moment the chair viciously attacked his right leg.

The instant Joe vaulted out of his chair with a yowl, his mug clattering to the floor, spilling tea everywhere, Alicia knew what had happened.

"Rosie!" she scolded, leaning down—not an easy thing to do these days—to peer under the table.

The orange tabby cat sat in the corner, looking pleased with herself.

"Rosie?" Joe followed Alicia's example, bending over to see his assailant for himself.

Alicia shook her finger. "Shame on you, Rosie Harris."

The cat looked at Joe and hissed.

"What sort of demon is that?"

"She's not a demon. Strangers make her nervous."

Joe straightened. "They make *her* nervous? *She's* the one with claws."

Alicia sat up. "She'll be okay once she gets used to you."

"She'd better." He scowled. "Got a mop? I'll clean up this mess."

"I'll do it. She's my cat." She started to rise, but he stopped her with a hand on her shoulder.

"No, I'll do it. Just tell me where the mop is."

"In the utility room."

"Any more cats lying in wait to take pieces out of me?"

She shook her head. "No more cats. But there's an overly friendly sheepdog in the backyard. I'll introduce you to Rags later."

"Great," he muttered as he turned away. "Just great."

Alicia bit her lip to keep from laughing out loud.

"Go ahead," he said without looking at her. "Laugh all you want. What goes around comes around."

"So I've heard."

Joe knew there was a good reason he'd lived the past two decades without owning a pet. With his left hand grasping the mop handle, he leaned down to check his right calf. He wouldn't be surprised if he found it bleeding. It wasn't, but there were a couple of thin red welts.

"This is a mistake and I'm going to regret it," he muttered.

It wasn't too late, of course. He could tell Alicia he'd changed his mind. Nothing irreversible had happened yet.

He came out of the utility room door and stopped still, captured by the view before him.

Alicia leaned back in one of those ugly fifties chairs that looked as if they were straight out of a trolley car diner. She stroked her belly with both hands, a tender smile curving her bowlike mouth.

"Humphrey," she said softly, "you're gonna have to help teach Rosie some manners when you get here. I don't seem to be doing much of a job of it."

Humphrey. What kind of name was that to call a kid? The baby was likely to be born with a textbook full of classic neuroses. It would take years of counseling to straighten him out.

As if she'd felt his gaze upon her, she glanced his way. Her smile vanished.

He was sorry to see it go. "Found it." He held up the mop. "Is it safe to come out?"

It worked. She smiled again. "Yes. Rosie's gone."

"You sure?" He poked his head around the edge of the door, pretending to be nervous.

"I'm sure." She pushed up from her chair. "While you do that, I'll make sure everything's ready for you in the baby's room. There's a twin-size bed in there for you to use."

"Hey, Alicia."

She stopped and looked over her shoulder.

"I planned on staying at a motel until your grandfather arrives. But I could use a place to store my stuff."

"I've got a room for storage upstairs. You can put most of it there. But you'll need some things in my bedroom and bathroom." She blushed the way she had that day in the café. "You know, so Grandpa won't suspect anything."

"I have a bad feeling about all of this."

"Are you trying to back out?"

As everyone in the world knew—judging by the countless jokes he'd heard over the past decade—lawyers were cold, calculating scavengers, the bottom-feeders of society, out to cut whoever's throat they must. But Joe didn't feel cold or calculating when she looked at him the way she was now. Instead, he felt like some chivalrous knight riding out to protect the fair damsel in distress.

Which was about the most *absurd* thing he'd ever thought!

"No," he answered as he turned away and applied the mop to the floor. "I made a promise and I'll keep it. But I think this is all one big mistake."

They had three days to learn everything they could about each other. Alicia knew it wasn't much time.

"We must *seem* as though we're in love," she said as they sat down that evening to a supper of green salad, spaghetti and garlic bread. "If we've been married for nearly eight months, we should have some sort of routine worked out." She reached for the salt shaker. "So tell me. Are you a morning person or a night person?"

"Night."

"I love mornings. I'm all sunshine and singing."

"That's sick." He tore off a piece of garlic bread. "My turn. Do you drink herbal tea because you like it or because you're pregnant?"

"Both. But I prefer coffee in the morning." She twirled spaghetti around her fork. "My doctor's name is Jamison. Matt Jamison. He's a general practitioner, and he's been my doctor for eight years."

"Why didn't you take my name when we got married?"

"That's a good point. Grandpa Roger will ask that, too." She pondered the matter for a few moments while eating. "I suppose we could use the excuse of all the red tape the store would have to go through."

"What kind of store is it, by the way? I've forgotten what your profile said."

"It's called Bundles of Joy, and it's a maternity and baby shop."

Joe raised an eyebrow as he straightened in his chair. "You're kidding."

"No. Not kidding."

"How long have you been in business?"

"For five years. I moved the store to the Main Street location three years ago. It's one block from the coffee shop where we met last week." She frowned. "Didn't we cover any of this after we connected on LinkedIn?"

"Some. But we'd better go over it again and again."

Alicia had a suspicion that Joe was beginning to enjoy himself. Perhaps this was a little like preparing for a trial. She could almost see the wheels in his head turning.

"What's the story about how we became reacquainted?" he asked. "And what are you telling your grandfather about why you kept the marriage a secret all this time?"

Her appetite, normally robust, was gone. She pushed her plate away, then slid her chair back from the table and rose. She walked to the window. A nearly full moon peeked over the mountains in the east. In a short while, it would be almost as bright as day outside.

She hated the idea of lying to Grandpa Roger, but what else could she do? He didn't need stress right now, not with his health so fragile. She remembered how he'd looked in that hospital room with machines beeping and fluids dripping through tubes. It was nothing short of a miracle that he was alive today, and he wasn't out of danger yet.

No, she didn't have any other choice. She would tell a thousand lies if she had to. She would pretend to be married and happy. To protect Grandpa Roger, she would do anything.

Joe touched her shoulder.

Surprised—she hadn't heard his approach—she turned quickly.

"You okay?" he asked, his voice gentle and low, his eyes watching her with concern.

She nodded, feeling weepy.

"Maybe we've covered enough for tonight. We can start again in the morning."

"Thanks for doing this, Joe." She swallowed the lump in her throat. "I can't say it enough. Thanks. I know it's an imposition."

He grinned. "I don't know. Free rent for six weeks. Somebody to talk to over a great supper of spaghetti. What's an imposition about that?"

"But it is, and we both know it."

"Hey." He leaned a little closer, laying the flat of his hand against her cheek. "What're old friends for?"

Her heart leaped in her chest. Her breath felt short.

Joe's eyes widened a fraction, then he stepped back from her. Looking over his shoulder toward the table, he said, "I'll clear up. You go on to bed. I can let myself out."

"You don't have to—"

"I'm used to doing dishes, Alicia. I've been taking care of myself for a lot of years."

She should ask him about his own brief marriage. It was something a second wife would know. But that could wait for another time.

"Go on." He jerked his head toward the doorway. "I'll make sure everything's locked up and the lights turned out." He smiled again. "See you in the morning. I'll be here bright and early."

She half wished he would take her in his arms. Then common sense returned.

"Good night," she whispered and hurried out of the kitchen.

"That went well, Palermo."

This knight-in-shining-armor gig wasn't as easy as it looked.

Joe cleared the table, setting dirty dishes on the counter and putting leftovers in the fridge. Then he filled the deep sink with hot sudsy water and washed the dishes, setting them in the drain to air-dry.

All the while he thought about Alicia, her love for her grandfather, and what a predicament she was in because of some jerk named Grant. Of course, that part was her own fault. Nobody with a lick of sense got married three weeks after meeting someone.

He thought of Marlene. His ex-wife. He and Marlene had known each other for four years before they got married, and their marriage hadn't lasted much longer than Alicia's. Only six months, but those had been the longest six months of Joe's life.

He winced. Joe Palermo, hotshot attorney, tops in his class—and major stooge. His ex-wife had taken him to the cleaners. Worse than the financial aspects of the divorce, however, had been the loss of his faith. He'd wanted to be married for a lifetime. Why hadn't God kept Marlene from leaving and divorcing him? He'd kept up his side of the bargain. Why hadn't God? He'd stayed angry about it for a long time.

He wasn't angry with God anymore. He'd come to accept that failures come to everyone, that bad things happen to good people, that even when you want something that is right, it doesn't mean you'll get it. He was learning to trust God with his days, with his future.

One thing he believed without question: marriage wasn't for him. He was content to return to an empty house at the end of the day. Like his dad before him, he immersed himself in work. That wouldn't change because he relocated from California to Idaho. And, when he wasn't working, he intended to hit the ski slopes or hike in the backcountry.

No, he wasn't—and wouldn't ever be—family man material.

He glanced around the bright yellow kitchen with all its cozy touches. Could he see himself living in a home like this?

Not hardly.

He hung up the dish towel, flicked off the light switch and headed out the door.

"Oh, Humphrey," Alicia whispered, "what's going on?"

Lying on her bed beneath her warm down comforter, she stared upward, watching as moonlight and shadows danced across her ceiling.

Rags whimpered and laid her head on the bed near Alicia's side. She ruffled the Old English sheepdog's ears.

"How about you, girl? You have any ideas?"

The dog plopped both of her front paws on the bed and began wagging her tail.

"Okay. For a little while."

Rags jumped onto the mattress and plopped down next to her mistress.

Alicia didn't know whether to laugh or cry. There she was, big, pregnant, single and in bed with her dog.

If that wasn't a commentary on her life, she didn't know what was.

Rags flopped her furry head onto Alicia's abdomen and whimpered again.

"My thoughts exactly," she whispered to the dog. "My thoughts exactly."

Chapter Three

Joe pulled his car into Alicia's driveway at seven-thirty the next morning. He'd looked for a Starbucks on the way but had come up empty. He hoped Alicia had made a pot of coffee. He needed caffeine in a bad way.

He rang the doorbell and waited—and waited. He'd figured she would be up since she claimed to be a morning person. He was about to ring the bell again when a large dog galloped into view around the corner of the house. The next thing Joe knew, the dog was up on its hind legs and its giant paws slammed against his chest, knocking him against the doorjamb.

"Hey!"

The dog slapped him in the face with a sloppy-wet tongue.

"Rags, no. Bad girl." Alicia stepped onto the

porch and shoved the dog away from Joe. "Get down. Get away. Bad girl."

He drew his arm across his face, wiping away the dog slobber.

"I'm sorry." Alicia choked on what sounded like a giggle, then tried to hide it by saying again, "I'm *so* sorry. I didn't know Rags was out. I told you she's overly affectionate. She loves people."

Joe glared at the dog. Rags sat with her head tipped to one side, her eyes obscured by that ridiculous mop of hair. Joe suspected the canine was grinning at him.

"She wouldn't hurt you," Alicia added. "Honest."

"Oh, really?" He turned his glare on her.

Her lips quivered, and the twinkle of amusement in her eyes was unmistakable.

"You think its funny?"

"I'm sorry. It's just…it's just…" She covered her mouth with one hand. "If you could've seen the two of you as I did when I opened the door."

"Oh, yeah. A regular comedy team."

"I'm sorry."

"Okay. Enough with the apologies." He drew a deep breath. "I need some coffee."

She stepped out of his way, allowing him to walk past her and was wise enough not to follow immediately.

In the kitchen Joe found an oversize mug on the counter next to the coffeepot. He filled it to the brim, then turned and leaned against the counter while taking his first sip of the dark brew.

Ambrosia!

Alicia Harris knew how to make good coffee. That was some consolation.

He took another sip, then released a deep sigh.

"The way you like it?" she asked from the doorway.

"Yeah." He looked toward her. "It's good."

"You said you're not a morning person. Would you rather I left you alone?"

"Not much point in it now."

She gave him a tentative smile, and he suspected she was about to start apologizing again.

He spoke before she could. "What's on the agenda for today?"

"I thought I'd take you into the shop. Introduce you to my employees."

She was wearing those silly bunny slippers, along with a soft-ribbed bathrobe in the same shade of pink. Her hair had a mussed, just-got-up look about it.

The women Joe had dated over the past decade would rather die than be seen like this. If asked, he'd have said he preferred it that way. Now he wasn't so sure. There was something appealing about Alicia in that getup.

He gave his head a slight shake, as if denying the thought. "I assume your employees are among the few who know the truth."

"Yes. There wasn't any way around it."

He nodded.

"But I can trust them."

He chose not to explain how the risk of discovery grew with every person who knew. If they wanted to pull off this charade, they'd better keep Grandpa Roger as close to home as they could.

"I did decide what to tell my grandfather." Alicia raked the fingers of one hand through her already-tousled hair. "About why I've kept our marriage a secret. I'm going to say I was so angry after my fight with him that I didn't tell him out of spite. Then when he got sick, I decided to wait until he was better. And after he said he was coming for a visit, I simply waited to surprise him. I'll say I didn't want to give him any sudden shocks over the phone."

"Do you think he'll buy it? That's a mighty flimsy story."

"I know." Her shoulders slumped. "But I thought it was better to stick as close to the truth as possible."

"Did you ever mention Grant's name to him?"

"Yes. When I told him I was getting married. But that was months ago and only one conversation that ended badly. If he remembers, I'll say he misunderstood me."

"Grant Reeves. Joe Palermo. Oh, sure. I see how he could confuse the two."

She started to cry.

He felt like a heel.

"We…I…we…have to make…this work," she blubbered.

Joe set down his mug and went to her, gathered her into his arms and held her close. "I'm sorry." He patted her back. "I didn't mean to be sarcastic. Don't worry. We'll carry this off. I did theater in high school. Remember? You came with Belinda to one of my plays. I'll be a fine actor. Your grandpa will never suspect a thing."

Alicia allowed herself to sink into the safety of Joe's embrace. It felt good to lean on someone else. She was tired of being strong and courageous.

But self-indulgence was a momentary thing. She couldn't let it last.

She placed her palms against his chest and gently pushed herself away. "I seem to be crying all the time. I don't suppose you'd believe me if I told you this isn't normal." She wiped the tears from her cheeks.

"I guess I bring out the worst in you."

"No, I think we can blame this on Humphrey."

"Good ol' Humphrey."

She tried to smile, but the attempt was weak.

"Go wash your face." He motioned toward the hall. "When you're ready, I'll take you out for breakfast before we head into town."

She didn't argue. It was more prudent to beat a hasty retreat.

But retreating from whom?

Joe Palermo or herself?

"Wow!" Susie Notter, the assistant manager at Bundles of Joy, rolled her eyes at Alicia. "You gotta give me directions to one of those social-networking sites if *he's* an example of the kind of guy you find there."

Alicia poked the young woman in the ribs with her elbow. "Shh. He'll hear you."

"Well, when you're through playing house with him," Susie whispered, "you can tell Mr. Palermo I've got a spare room he's welcome to. And he won't even have to meet any of my family."

A number of terse responses popped into Alicia's head. She bit her tongue to keep from saying them.

Joe turned from the wall of stuffed animals he'd been inspecting. He held up a furry seal. "Looks like an appropriate toy for a kid called Humphrey. Don't you think?"

Her heart did a somersault, leaving her unable to speak. The best she could do was smile and nod in response.

"Does your husband get a store discount?" he asked.

My husband...

Susie answered for her. "Of course he does. Come over here, Mr. Palermo, and I'll ring up your purchase."

Joe was just a childhood friend from the old

neighborhood. Nothing more. She didn't want him to be anything more than that. Therefore, these feelings meant nothing.

She had to remember she'd fallen hard and fast for Grant, and look where it got her. Not that she was sorry about having this baby, but she did regret the circumstances surrounding it. She believed in marriage, the Ward-and-June-Cleaver kind of household, two-point-three kids, the whole "American dream" bit.

She placed a hand on her abdomen. "Sorry, Humphrey," she said softly. "It would be nice to have a daddy, but we'll do the best we can on our own."

Joe turned from the cash register, purchase in hand. His grin was still in place, and it stole her breath a second time.

"How about I take you to lunch?" he asked.

She doubted she could eat a bite. "It's not that long since we had breakfast."

"Well, I'm hungry." He walked toward her, took hold of her arm, then glanced over his shoulder. "Nice to meet you, Susie." He looked in the other direction. "You, too, Judy," he said to the other salesperson.

With that, he guided Alicia toward the front door.

It took some doing, but Joe managed to shake Alicia free from whatever strange mood had overtaken her.

Over a lunch of clam chowder and corn bread,

they reminisced about the old days when they'd been neighbors in a middle-class Meridian neighborhood. They laughed often, their conversation filled with the words *Do you remember...?* Alicia even confessed she'd had a crush on him when she was little and had wanted him to be the first boy to kiss her. He grinned when he heard that, liking the idea more than he should.

"Must have been fate that I saw your name on LinkedIn."

"I couldn't believe it when that message came through from you. I'd only completed my profile about a week before. And I did that only because a friend told me it was good for business reasons to be on there."

"I'm glad you listened to your friend. It felt good, seeing your name, thinking back to the old neighborhood. Growing up in Idaho gave me the best kind of childhood."

"Me, too."

"You know what's surprised me most about you? When you talk about what happened with Grant, you never sound the least bit bitter." He thought of the bitterness he'd carried around after his own divorce. "It could have soured you on all men, what he did to you."

Her smile faded. "All men didn't have anything to do with this. It was between me and Grant, and I was at fault, too." She tipped her head to one side.

"How about you? Did your ex-wife sour you on all women?"

"Maybe not on all women, but I don't plan on ever walking down the aisle again. Marriage isn't for me." He wished he'd never introduced the topic.

"You don't want to have children of your own?"

"No." He shook his head. "I wouldn't make a good father. I'm too much like my old man. He didn't have time for the kids he had. A workaholic shouldn't have children. It makes things tough on everyone involved."

"And you're a workaholic?"

"With a capital *W*."

"How sad," she said in a low voice. Then, "Maybe we should go. I've got grocery shopping to do. I'm picking up the turkey today."

Joe rose and stepped around the table to pull out her chair, offering his hand to help her to her feet. As she stood, her shoulder rubbed against him. He caught a whiff of her musky cologne. Her aquamarine eyes seemed darker than usual as she met his gaze. The restaurant sounds faded into the distance.

She wasn't ten, and he wouldn't be the first, but he wouldn't mind kissing her now.

Alicia blushed, as if she'd read his thoughts.

If he wasn't careful, he'd forget this was all pretend. He'd make an A number one fool out of himself.

He let go of her hand. "I'll pay the bill and meet you at the front door."

He walked away without a backward glance, hoping it wasn't already too late to avoid playing the fool.

By the time the two of them returned home, Alicia was exhausted. The grocery store had been jam-packed. It seemed she wasn't the only one who waited until Thanksgiving week to do her shopping. Big mistake. The lines had been long, the checkout clerks frazzled.

It didn't help that every time she looked at Joe she remembered the moment when she'd thought he might kiss her. Worse yet, she remembered wanting him to.

Joe had just brought in the last two canvas shopping bags and set them on the kitchen counter when the phone rang.

"Hello?" Alicia answered.

"Hello, my girl."

"Grandpa? Is something wrong?"

"Does something have to be wrong for me to call you?"

"No. It's just, you'll be here in a couple of days, and I didn't expect—"

"Are you going to fuss over me like one of those confounded nurses the whole time I'm there?"

"Yes." She smiled, envisioning the elderly man with the perpetual twinkle in his eyes.

"Okay. Now that *that's* settled, the reason I called

was to tell you my itinerary has changed. I'll be in an hour earlier on Wednesday. Nice surprise, isn't it?"

"Yes, it is."

Joe watched her with a look that caused her heart to flutter.

"Grandpa, I've got a surprise for you, too." She glanced at her belly. "A couple of them."

"What?"

"I don't want to tell you over the phone. You'll have to wait until you get here."

"Teasing your grandpa, are you?"

"Maybe a little." She lowered her voice. "I love you."

"I love you, too."

"I'm looking forward to your visit. Very much."

"Me, too. So I'll see you at the airport on Wednesday. One o'clock instead of two. Same flight number."

"I'll be there with bells on."

"Goodbye, dear. See you soon."

"Bye, Grandpa."

The connection was broken, and Alicia hung up the phone.

"Everything okay?"

She turned toward him. "Yes." But the fluttering in her heart when she met his gaze made her wonder if she spoke the truth.

Chapter Four

Alicia was shaking. Whether from excitement or nerves, Joe couldn't be sure. He suspected it was a combination of the two.

As passengers exited the concourse, Joe placed an arm around her back and whispered, "Here we go, sweetheart."

She glanced up, obviously surprised by the endearment.

"The charade begins," he added, wanting her to understand his choice of words was part of the pretense. "Act 1, scene 1. Remember your lines?"

She gave him a pained smile, accompanied by a nod, then returned her gaze to the concourse.

The waiting area grew noisier as friends and family were welcomed.

"There he is!" Alicia raised an arm and waved. "Grandpa! Over here!"

Roger Harris hadn't changed much in the past two

decades. Perhaps the good reverend was a bit thinner, but his hair was the same stone-gray and his smile was as warm and friendly as Joe remembered. In fact, he would say her grandfather looked good for a man of seventy-seven who'd survived a heart attack.

There was a question in the older man's eyes as he approached the two of them. Then he stopped short, his eyes widening, and Joe knew Roger Harris had finally noticed Alicia's expanded waistline.

"Hi, Grandpa." Her greeting was tentative.

Joe tightened his arm and urged her forward with a gentle pressure.

"I assume *this*—" Grandpa Roger glanced at her belly "—is part of my surprise?"

"Yes." She took a deep breath. "And here is the other part. This is Joe Palermo. My husband."

Joe offered his hand. "Nice to see you, sir."

Grandpa Roger hesitated only a moment before taking Joe's hand in his. "And you, young man." His gaze was as firm as his grasp. "Have we met before?"

"Years ago, Mr. Harris. When I was a kid. I lived across the street from Alicia until my dad transferred to California. I came back to Idaho to enjoy the simpler life."

Grandpa Roger nodded, then looked at his granddaughter once again. "I think it's time for a hug. The rest of the story can wait."

She responded immediately, throwing her arms around him and holding on tight. Her grandfather said something to her, but he spoke too softly for

Joe to understand. When the older man looked at him over Alicia's shoulder, Joe felt a sudden desire to earn his respect.

He wondered if that would be possible, given the lies he intended to tell.

While Joe carried her grandfather's luggage into the house, Alicia put the kettle on for tea.

"Are you hungry, Grandpa? It'll be an hour before dinner's ready."

"I'm not in any hurry. But I would like to hear more about you and Joe."

She'd known she couldn't put off this discussion for long.

"Why did you keep the marriage a secret from me?"

She turned. Her grandfather was seated on one of the kitchen chairs, watching her with those kind, loving eyes of his. She hated lying to him, even if it was for his own good.

He patted his hand on the table. "Come sit down. Come talk to me."

"Okay," she answered softly as she obeyed.

"Are you happy?"

"Yes." She smiled to prove it, but inside she quivered.

"Then tell me."

"Remember our argument when I told you I was getting married after a whirlwind romance?"

He nodded.

"I was so angry, I decided not to tell you I got married, despite your advice to wait awhile. It was silly and petty of me, I know, but that was my reason for keeping it a secret." She looked down at her hands, unable to meet his gaze while she spun her tale of half-truths and outright lies. "When I discovered I was pregnant, I knew I had to tell you, but I kept putting it off because I was ashamed of the way I'd acted. Then you got sick and I couldn't tell you until you were better. And...well...here you are." She ended with a slight shrug.

"Here I am."

She looked up. "I'm sorry, Grandpa. I didn't mean for it to happen this way."

"But you *are* happy?"

"Yes, I'm happy."

"And the baby? When is it due?"

"January 20."

"My first great-grandchild. I wish your grandmother could have lived to see this."

Her heart tightened. "Me, too."

Joe entered the kitchen at that moment. He hesitated in the doorway, then strode across the room, coming to a stop behind Alicia's chair. He placed his hands on her shoulders, leaned down and kissed the top of her head.

A shiver raced through her.

"I put the bags on the bed, sir, and hung you suit in the closet."

"Thank you." Her grandfather motioned to another chair. "No time like the present to get acquainted. I've forgotten if Alicia told me what you do for a living."

"I'm an attorney."

Alicia noticed how calm Joe looked and sounded. She wished she felt the same.

"What sort of law do you practice?"

"Corporate, mostly, but I do some trial work, too."

"What firm are you with?"

Alicia felt a stab of alarm. They hadn't discussed any of this.

Grandpa Roger shook his head. "It sounds like I'm interrogating you, doesn't it?"

"I don't mind, sir. And to answer your question, I'm not with any local firm as yet. I'm wrapping up some things for clients in California while working out of the house. I may be settled into a new firm by January, but I'm not in any hurry. I wouldn't mind being at home when our baby arrives."

Our baby... Alicia imagined him holding a newborn in his arms.

"It'd give us more time to bond. My father worked such long hours, I hardly knew him. I'd like things to be different with my kid."

"Wonderful sentiment," her grandfather said. "And with laptops, faxes and email, I guess no one has to have an outside office these days."

"No, sir. That's true."

The kettle began to whistle. Alicia rose from her chair, excusing herself with a mumbled apology, glad for a moment to collect her thoughts. The way Joe had talked about bonding with his child and how he hadn't known his own father had left her oddly disturbed. She'd found herself believing him, caught up in the fantasy they were spinning for her grandfather.

"Do you need any help, sweetheart?"

She knew her cheeks were flushed as she turned to answer Joe. "No, thanks. I've got it." She carried the teacups to the table and set one before her grandfather, the other before Joe.

"She's still trying to get me to drink this herbal stuff," Joe said with a chuckle as his gaze met hers. "Even after all these months together, she hasn't given up."

Dropping through a hole in the floor would have been a convenient escape. It didn't happen.

"Alicia's always been a headstrong girl," Grandpa Roger said. "Mind of her own. I suppose you know I advised her against marrying in such a hurry."

"Yes, sir. So I heard." Joe glanced at the older man. "I'd like you to know, right up front, that keeping the news about our wedding and the baby from you was her idea. Not mine. I told her it was better to tell the truth."

Alicia wanted to kick him.

All things considered, the evening went well.

Over a supper of grilled chicken breasts, mashed potatoes, and peas with carrots, Alicia asked her grandfather about his friends in Arizona, about the heart specialist's recommendations for his diet, about anything that would steer the conversation away from Joe and their "marriage."

It wasn't yet nine o'clock when Grandpa Roger announced it was time for him to turn in.

"Are you feeling all right?" she asked, suddenly anxious.

"A bit tired, is all. It's been a long day." He rose from the easy chair where he'd been sitting. "I'll see you both in the morning. Good night."

"Good night," Alicia and Joe said in unison.

She waited until she heard the bedroom door close before she asked, "Do you think he's really all right? I should have insisted he lie down when we first got home."

"Alicia…" Joe laid his hand on her shoulder. "Relax. He said he was just tired."

"I know, but—"

He squeezed her shoulder. "He's okay."

She looked at him. The hint of a smile curved his mouth, and his gaze was filled with tenderness. She hoped she wasn't going to start crying again. She was sick to death of her propensity for turning on the waterworks.

"Maybe I'd better go to bed, too." She stood. "I'll be up early to put the turkey in the oven."

"I'm going to watch a bit of television."

She nodded.

He lowered his voice. "I'll wait until Roger's had time to fall asleep, then I'll let myself into the nursery. But how will I know when it's okay for me to come through your room in the morning?"

"I brought home a two-way baby monitoring system so we can talk to each other. They work like walkie-talkies."

"Good thinking."

She smiled. "Good night then. I hope that bed isn't too miserable."

"It'll be fine. See you in the morning."

Joe flicked through the local channels but didn't find anything worth watching. In California, he'd had a satellite system, complete with more channels than he'd known what to do with. Alicia didn't even have basic cable.

Alicia...

He glanced toward the master bedroom. No light showed beneath the door. She must be in bed, but he'd bet money she wasn't asleep yet. She'd been stretched tight as a drum all day. He wished he knew how to make her relax.

But she wasn't his responsibility, he reminded himself. This whole charade was her problem. He would do his part as best he could, but he couldn't fix everything. He sure couldn't make her feel better about it.

"Never should've agreed to this," he muttered as he got to his feet, at the same time clicking off the TV with the remote control.

After checking the lock on the front door, he put out the last light and made his way toward the bathroom.

* * *

Through the monitor, Alicia listened to the almost undetectable sounds of Joe moving around in the nursery. She hoped he didn't stub his toe in the dark. That room had become something of a catchall in recent months.

Rosie must have heard the sounds, too, for she hissed at the nightstand.

"Be good, Rosie," Alicia whispered. "I need you to be nice to Joe." She stroked the cat's fur.

Through the monitor came a low, male voice. "Tell her if she isn't nice to me, next time I'll scratch back."

She laughed—the tension easing from her shoulders—as she reached for the monitor, discovering that the button she needed to hold down in order to be heard in the other room was stuck. She would have to be careful about that in the future.

"Good night, Joe."

"Night, Alicia."

It was going to be all right. They would make it through Thanksgiving and Christmas. Grandpa Roger would go home, none the wiser but in good health. Joe would find a new law firm and a new place to live. Maybe they would even stay friends. She hoped so.

More than she should.

Chapter Five

Daylight peeked through the nursery windows when Joe opened his eyes the following morning. He hadn't slept this soundly in ages.

Through the closed door, he heard voices. Roger and Alicia must be up. Why hadn't she told him to do the same? The monitor worked well enough last night.

He got up, pulled on his jeans and a T-shirt, and then made sure to remove all evidence that he'd been in the room. Finally, he made his way on bare feet out the exterior nursery door onto the porch and in through the door into Alicia's bedroom. Once inside, he stopped and looked around.

The room seemed to fit Alicia. It had an old-world charm about it, from the four-poster bed to the large wardrobe with claw-feet and its matching dressing table and chest of drawers.

More sounds reached him, and he realized he

needed to get out there and play his part. Didn't want Grandpa Roger thinking him a laggard. He opened the bottom drawer and removed clean clothes. Then he opened the door to the hallway and closed it behind him, this time making sure he would be heard. From there he went into the bathroom. Fifteen minutes later, he emerged—showered, shaved and ready for his coffee.

"Good morning," he said as he entered the kitchen. He stopped behind Alicia's chair, leaned down and kissed the back of her neck. "Sorry I overslept. I meant to help you get the turkey in the oven."

"It's okay." She didn't quite meet his gaze when she looked up. "I could see you were tired." Her cheeks were flushed.

Joe looked toward her grandfather. "Good morning, sir. Did you sleep well?"

"I certainly did. That's a comfortable bed in the guest room."

Grandpa Roger slid his chair back from the table. "I'd better take my walk before the day gets away from me."

"Do you mind company?" Joe asked. "I could use some fresh air to wake me up."

"I'd be delighted, son. I'll get my coat."

"Are you crazy?" Alicia asked in a whisper the instant her grandfather was out of hearing. "Why did you volunteer to go with him? He'll end up asking you more questions."

"It can't be avoided. Might as well get used to it. It'll look more suspicious if I avoid him."

"Okay. Just don't stay out too long. And for goodness' sake, keep your stories straight."

The sky was one of those crystal clear winter blues that almost hurt the eyes. The temperature hovered around freezing, and the two men could see their breath as they ambled down the quiet country road. The Boise Mountains to the north and the Owyhee Mountains to the south wore cloaks of white, and despite the cloudless day, there was a promise of snowfall in the air.

"I miss winter, living in Arizona," Grandpa Roger said, breaking the self-imposed silence that had stretched between them.

"That's how I felt about California. I mean, all that sunshine's great for the sun worshippers, but that was never my scene. Give me the slopes any day of the week."

Alicia's grandfather glanced at Joe. "Alicia never cared much for skiing. Think she'll take it up now?"

"I don't know." He made a mental note to ask her. "But I'll do my best to change her mind."

"Well, it won't be this year."

"No, sir. It won't."

They continued in silence a short while longer.

"Joe?"

"Yes, sir?"

"Except for you now, I'm all the family Alicia's

got. While I hope the good Lord will give me plenty more years on this earth, I'd like to know she's in good hands if I'm called home anytime soon."

"You can depend on me to take care of her, sir." He hadn't expected the lie to come so hard. "I'll see she doesn't go in want of anything." Maybe it didn't have to be a lie. Just because he wasn't married to Alicia Harris didn't mean he couldn't check on her every now and again, make certain she and the baby were okay.

The elderly man smiled. "Why don't you call me Roger or Grandpa? There shouldn't be all this formality between us. You and I are family, and you're about to make me a great-grandfather."

"No, sir."

Grandpa Roger chuckled.

Joe grinned. "Sorry."

Another stretch of silence followed. Joe was surprised by how comfortable it felt. As if he and the older man had spent many such hours together.

"Tell me more about how you and Alicia became reacquainted. On the internet, I understood, but beyond a bit of shopping online and email, I can't say I'm familiar with all the newfangled things that exist."

"We met on a business-networking site. It's used for lots of different reasons. We met because of our Idaho connections. I don't even remember how I stumbled on her name, but once we determined we were the same Joe Palermo and Alicia Harris that grew up on the same street, things just sort of escalated from there." So far, so good. Everything he'd said was the truth.

"Maybe you could give me a few lessons about those networking sites. I may be an old dog, but I can still learn a few new tricks."

"Sure. I'd be glad to. I'll pull out my laptop any time you're ready."

Alicia stepped to the front room windows and looked outside. Relief flooded through her when she saw Grandpa Roger and Joe coming up the walk. They both looked calm and comfortable. Apparently there'd been no slipup on Joe's part.

She opened the door as they ascended the porch steps. "Are you frozen yet?"

"Not at all," her grandfather replied. "It's a lovely morning."

"Brr." She shuddered. "Too cold for my blood."

Joe stopped in front of her and kissed her cheek. Her heart missed a beat, and her breath caught in her chest.

"Did I say how pretty you look this morning?" he whispered. "I expect this is going to be the best Thanksgiving I've ever had."

A pleasant warmth surged through her veins.

A half second later she realized her grandfather was watching them and grinning from ear to ear. Of course. Joe was doing this for Grandpa Roger's benefit. She'd almost forgotten it was an act. For a moment she'd become part of the fantasy.

"Do you need any help in the kitchen?" Joe continued.

She shook her head, her mouth too dry to speak.

"Good. I promised your grandfather I'd give him a lesson on the Internet." He smiled that sexy smile of his. "Maybe he'll meet an old friend online and end up as happy as we are."

Joe gave her another kiss, this time on the forehead. Then he strode toward the bedroom, whistling softly.

She stood beside the open door a moment or two longer, thankful for the cool air on her skin. Her head told her his words were nothing more than lines, but her heart longed to believe they were true.

She was embarrassed to admit, even to herself, how ridiculously eager for a man's compliments she was.

Hormones again, she decided as she closed the door. Just these stupid hormones.

"Hey, Alicia," Joe called from the bedroom. "Can you come here a minute?"

"Coming." She headed for the hallway. "I'll be right back, Grandpa."

When she entered the master bedroom, she found Joe on his knees beside the chest of drawers.

"Lose something?" she asked.

"Yeah. My favorite pen. I keep it in the side pocket of my briefcase. I used it yesterday morning, but it isn't there now." He straightened, sitting back on his heels. "It's a marbled navy-blue color with a gold band. About this wide." He indicated the width with his right thumb and index finger. "Have you seen it?"

She shook her head. "Sorry."

He stood. "I suppose it'll turn up eventually." He stepped closer to her and lowered his voice. "How come you don't like to snow ski?"

"What?"

"Your grandfather says you don't like to ski."

"No, I don't."

"Why?"

His eyes were a luscious shade of brown. When he looked at her, so intent and earnest, she could hardly think straight.

"Alicia?"

She swallowed. "I didn't care for it, the times I've tried."

"Maybe you had the wrong instructor." He smiled as he tipped his head to one side. "Do you suppose you'd give it another try for your husband?"

There went her heart, thumping erratically again.

"After the baby comes, of course," Joe went on.

He didn't have a clue how his words affected her. How could he? She wasn't sure *she* understood.

"But that's only..." He paused. "What? Less than eight weeks now?"

Somehow she found her voice. "I'm sure the season will be nearly over before the doctor would release me to go skiing."

"I know that. But your grandfather was wondering if you might take it up now that we're married, and I thought I'd better find out. Seems like something we would've talked about. Doesn't it?"

He had a way of bursting her bubbles before she got too carried away. She should be grateful for that.

"You're right, Joe. We should have talked about it. And the answer is, no. I don't want to take up skiing."

"Too bad." He looked disappointed. "I think you could've learned to like it."

She had the horrible feeling he was right. She thought she could learn to like anything he wanted to teach her.

"I'd better baste the turkey," she whispered, hurrying away before those sharp eyes of his saw more than she wanted them to.

Joe frowned as he set his laptop on a table. What had gotten into him? Had he forgotten this was an elaborate masquerade? He'd actually hoped Alicia would agree to go skiing with him sometime in the future. He'd been sorry when she refused him.

Too much time on my hands, he thought as he turned on the computer and watched it power up. "Time I got back to work."

"What's that?"

Joe looked over his shoulder at Alicia's grandfather. "Nothing. Just talking to myself."

"That's a sign of old age," Grandpa Roger said with a twinkle in his eyes.

"No doubt." He motioned to a chair. "Ready to begin?"

"I'm ready." The older man sat down.

"Great."

After about half an hour of preliminary instructions, Joe could see that this "old dog," as Grandpa Roger had called himself, was plenty quick to learn new tricks.

"Fascinating," Grandpa Roger said. "I've heard about sites like this on the news, but never visited them. Do you mind if I continue to surf for a while?"

"Not at all." Joe glanced toward the kitchen.

"Go ahead. See if she needs any help."

Joe hadn't meant to give the impression he was thinking about Alicia—even though he had been. With a nod, he rose from his chair and walked away. At the kitchen doorway, he paused. She stood near the sink, her hands folded atop her swollen belly, her expression wistful as she gazed out the window at the sunny day. She looked so…beautiful. So kissable. So feminine and warm and tender.

It felt right, being here in this house, watching Alicia move about the kitchen. It felt familiar, as if he'd been doing it for months. Crazy, but there it was. That's how he felt.

She turned her head and saw him standing there. She gave him a hesitant smile. "How's the lesson coming?"

"Fine. Your grandfather knows more than he let on, and he's quick to learn what he doesn't."

"Uh-huh."

The need to take her in his arms, to kiss her—
really kiss her—swept over him.

She checked her wristwatch, then crossed the
kitchen to the stove. Guessing her intent and wanting to be near, he followed her there.

"Let me do that for you. You shouldn't be lifting."

He drew on the oven mitts, removed the roasting
pan from the oven, then tipped it slightly to one side
so she could baste the bird.

"Thank you," she said without looking at him.

It was a good thing she didn't look up. She might
have seen what he was thinking, and that would be
a big mistake.

Chapter Six

Alicia arrived at the store an hour before it opened Friday morning. Like other retail businesses, Bundles of Joy relied on the day after Thanksgiving to make a hefty contribution to the profit margin for the year. She knew the day would be a long one and had warned both Joe and her grandfather not to expect her until ten o'clock that night.

"You shouldn't put in those kind of hours in your condition," Grandpa Roger had told her.

But what could she do? This was her livelihood. She was the boss. She had to be there.

Besides, this was the night of their special Father's Sale. From six to nine, the only females allowed in the store would be Alicia and her staff. This was an evening designed for husbands and fathers to come in and find those special gifts for their wives and children. Alicia had come up with the idea three years ago, and it had been a huge hit. Now it was an expected annual tradition.

In the back room she hung up her coat, then put her turkey sandwich in the small refrigerator before filling the coffeepot with water. By the time the coffee was done percolating, Susie had arrived.

"How was your Thanksgiving?" Susie shed her parka and draped it over a hanger.

"Very nice. How about yours?"

"Filling. I almost had to roll myself here from the parking lot. I eat way too much at these big family dinners."

Alicia grinned as she nodded in agreement.

"Your *husband* and grandfather getting along?" There was a mischievous gleam in Susie's eyes as she asked her question.

"Yes." Alicia envisioned the two men as they'd sat, side by side, last evening, continuing her grandfather's lessons on the internet. Two boys with their toys, she thought now. If things continued this way, they would be the best of friends in no time.

"So if they're getting along," Susie inquired, "why the frown?"

"Was I frowning?"

"You know it."

Alicia gave her head a tiny shake. "It isn't anything. I was just lost in thought."

"Hmm." Susie poured herself a cup of coffee. "Are you worried about what will happen today while you're gone? I mean, the two of them left to their own devices. Scary."

"No, I'm not worried." At least, she hadn't been until Susie suggested it.

What were Grandpa and Joe going to do while she was at work? Why hadn't she considered how often the two men would be together without her? She and Joe had covered a lot of territory, made up a lot of "facts," but there was no way she'd told him everything he should know. Their real history was only days long, not eight months.

Alicia groaned.

Susie was right. She *should* be worried.

The computer showroom was a madhouse.

Joe glanced sideways at Alicia's grandfather as the glass-and-chrome doors swung closed behind them. "Are you sure you want to do this today?"

"I'm sure."

"I'd be happy to pick one out and bring it home to you."

"Young man, I'm not about to spend my remaining years living in dread of another heart attack. I want to experience this for myself."

Alicia would kill Joe if anything happened to the old man, but he knew it was futile to try to change Grandpa Roger's mind. He'd already discovered where Alicia got her stubborn streak.

A salesman appeared before them. "Can I help you?"

"Yes," Joe answered. "We're looking for a laptop for my friend here."

"Right this way."

Joe motioned for Grandpa Roger to follow the salesman, then fell into step behind the older man. Above the din of conversations, he heard the salesman begin his pitch.

He wondered how Alicia's day was going. Was Bundles of Joy as jam-packed with customers as this showroom? He didn't know whether to hope so or not. She'd looked tired this morning. He suspected she wasn't sleeping well.

I wonder if it has anything to do with me.

He silently laughed at himself. What an absurd, egotistical notion! Why should he cause her to lose sleep? They were nothing to each other but friends.

And *I'm* the friend who finds her attractive.

"Joe?"

At the sound of Grandpa Roger's voice, he dragged his thoughts to the present. "Yeah?"

"You're the expert. What do you think?"

"Sorry. About what?"

The salesman did everything but roll his eyes in exasperation, then began his spiel a second time, enumerating all the advantages of the laptops on display.

An hour later, the two men left the store, their purchase made. Roger Harris was the brand-new owner of a lightweight, high-speed, state-of-the-art laptop computer. His eyes twinkled like a kid's on Christmas morning, and there was a definite spring in his step as they walked toward Joe's SUV.

"Let me buy you lunch," the older man offered. "We can have leftovers for supper."

"Sounds good to me. Where to?"

"How about Gracie's?"

Joe closed his door and stuck the key in the ignition. "Where's that?"

Grandpa Roger lifted an eyebrow. "You've been married eight months, and Alicia's never taken you to Gracie's?"

"We don't eat out much," Joe bluffed.

"I guess not."

He started the engine. "You point the way. I'll get us there. Maybe we can beat the lunch crowd."

Gracie's was one of those home-style restaurants found in every small town in America. It was in a converted brick house, nestled a block away from Meridian's main drag. A handicapped ramp had been added to the front entrance, and the backyard had been turned into a black-topped parking lot. Two ancient maple trees, their branches stripped bare by winter, stood as sentries on either side of the driveway.

They were too late to beat the lunch crowd, Joe realized as he pulled his vehicle into the only available spot. Or maybe they were too early to avoid the breakfast crowd. He couldn't be sure.

"Alicia, her grandmother and I used to come here the first Saturday of every month for breakfast,"

Grandpa Roger said. "It was a favorite tradition. Gracie serves the best French toast with homemade maple syrup you've ever eaten."

The two of them walked toward the entrance. After today, Joe planned to avoid this kind of thing like the plague. Ever since he'd sat in that Boise coffee shop two weeks ago and agreed to this crazy plan of Alicia's, he'd been doing things that were totally out of character. He'd better start acting like the work-obsessed attorney he was and forget this cozy-family make-believe world he'd been sucked into.

By the time he and Grandpa Roger were seated at a table near one of the gingham-curtained windows, Joe had managed to steer the conversation back to computers. He succeeded in keeping it there until midway through the meal.

"I'm curious about something," Alicia's grandfather began.

Joe tried not to let his apprehension show.

"Doesn't it bother you that Alicia didn't change her last name to Palermo?"

"Well..." he said slowly, trying for just the right tone. "Maybe a little. But these days it's common."

"It seems so unlike her. My granddaughter's always been a traditionalist. *And* a romantic." Grandpa Roger looked at Joe. "Only a romantic could fall in love and marry so quickly, right?"

"I guess so."

"Which means you must be a bit of a romantic yourself."

Joe Palermo? A romantic? When pigs fly.

He cleared his throat, then said, "We discussed it, of course. The name thing. It just made more sense, because of her business, to leave things as they were."

"I suppose." Grandpa Roger looked unconvinced. "Call me old-fashioned. I think a man and wife should share the same last name with their children. The baby will be a Palermo, after all."

"Humphrey Palermo?" Joe said beneath his breath—and then grinned at the ridiculous sound of it.

"Pardon?"

His grin broadened. "Nothing, sir. Just a private joke between Alicia and me."

The older man smiled, too. "Every marriage should have a few of those. Keeps you close."

Joe felt a stab of guilt. He and Alicia had fabricated a life, and Roger Harris had bought into it, hook, line and sinker. When her grandfather looked at the two of them, he saw a couple of romantics in love. He couldn't know—and hopefully would never know—how wrong he was.

"This is our first," the man said as he perused the racks of maternity wear. "We've been trying for over ten years to have a baby and just about gave up hope." His gaze shifted to Alicia's abdomen. "Your baby must be due about the same time as ours." He looked up. "January, right?"

Alicia nodded, smiling at him.

"Thought so." He paused, and his expression changed to one of desperation. "I want to buy her something pretty to wear for the holidays. We've got several nice parties to go to. You know, glittery business affairs. But she's feeling really unattractive right now and uncertain if she should even go."

Boy, could Alicia relate to that.

"She's not, though." The man's eyes shone with love, and his voice revealed the depths of his feelings. "She's beautiful. Especially now."

Alicia felt a lump forming in her throat. What would it be like to have someone feel that way about her?

"Janet's about your size and coloring. Can you recommend something?"

She forced another smile, then said, "Come with me. I think I have the dress you're looking for."

Her instincts proved correct. Her customer thought the sequined maternity dress with its long overjacket was perfect, and he left Bundles of Joy a happy man.

But no matter how many others Alicia waited on during the remaining hours of the Father's Sale, she couldn't shake the memory of that man—of Janet's husband—and the way he'd said his pregnant wife was beautiful. There was no denying the longing in her heart to experience a love like that for herself.

By the time she pulled into her driveway at nine forty-five that night, Alicia was in a full blue funk.

It didn't help that the house was mostly dark. Apparently no one had waited up for her. Rags greeted her by the back door. At least she could count on her trusty dog to be glad to see her. That was something.

In the kitchen Alicia set her purse and car keys on the counter, then checked her answering machine for messages. There were none. She found the mail on the kitchen table. Bills. Three applications for new credit cards. A slew of ads. One magazine. Nothing exciting.

Rosie jumped onto the table, demanding attention with a strident, *"Meow!"*

Alicia lifted her into her arms. "So what did everyone do today while I was working?"

The cat purred.

"You're a regular font of information."

Rosie rubbed the side of her head against Alicia's chest and purred more loudly.

"Whatever it was, it must have worn them out. It isn't even ten o'clock." She set the cat on the floor. "Personally, I'm ready for bed, too."

She flicked off the light switch and made her way toward her bedroom by the soft glow of several night lights, strategically placed throughout the house.

It didn't take her long to get ready for bed. She was a no-fuss kind of gal. Brush the teeth. Wash the face. Put on her comfy pajamas. Fall into the big four-poster and pull the thick down comforter up to her chin.

She closed her eyes and sighed deeply. Right at

this moment, with her feet hurting and her muscles aching, it was difficult to remember why she'd thought going into retail was a good idea.

The monitor made a slight puffy sound before Joe's voice came through the speaker. "That you, Alicia?"

The button was stuck again. She would have to exchange this two-way set and get one that worked properly before the baby arrived.

"It's me," she answered.

"You're home earlier than you thought."

"A little bit." She rolled onto her side and pulled the monitor closer. "You guys went to bed early, too."

"Yeah. Your grandpa's an early-to-bed sort of guy. I figured I might as well do the same."

She closed her eyes, a tired smile curving the corners of her mouth. It was kind of nice, lying here, talking to someone besides Rosie or Rags before she fell asleep.

"Alicia?"

"Yes?"

"I'm going to leave early in the morning for Bogus to ski. I heard today that they've got great powder for opening weekend."

She felt a sting of disappointment, a feeling she had no right to feel. "Okay."

"I'll fill you in on what your grandfather and I did today before I go."

"All right."

"Pleasant dreams."

"Good night, Joe."

Chapter Seven

Alicia was standing at the stove, frying bacon in a skillet, when Joe entered the kitchen. She saw him hesitate and check the room. Instinctively she knew that if her grandfather had been present Joe would have given her a kiss for a greeting. But since Grandpa Roger wasn't in the room, he stayed where he was.

"Morning. Smells good."

"The bacon's for you and me."

"Yeah. I figured." He walked over to her. "I'm missing one of my black leather driving gloves. You haven't seen it anywhere, have you?"

"No. Sorry, I haven't."

"Hope I haven't lost it."

"Where did you last have it?"

"When your grandpa and I got home. I took them off and left them on the table by the front door."

As he spoke, he moved toward the coffeepot. "This morning there's only one of them."

His hair looked as though he'd finger-combed it, and she'd already learned that his voice sounded a bit gravelly first thing in the morning. Seeing him, hearing him, made her pulse race.

This wasn't good. She'd reacted the same way around Joe when she was ten years old and harboring a giant-size crush on him. But she wasn't ten now. She had to remember that he was doing her a favor and nothing more.

"I think the bacon's done."

Alicia gasped and the fork dropped from her hand.

"Did you burn yourself?"

"No. No, I—" She clamped her mouth shut without finishing her sentence. She couldn't tell him what she'd been thinking.

Joe pulled the skillet off the burner, then scooped the overly crisp bacon onto a paper towel with a spatula.

By the time he was finished, Alicia felt a little more composed. "Thanks. My mind wandered."

He glanced over his shoulder. After a moment, he smiled.

There went her pulse again, skyrocketing.

"Have I told you how much I like your pink bunny slippers?" he asked softly. "They're very...*you*."

She wished her heart would stop fluttering like a captured bird. "That doesn't sound like much of a compliment," she whispered, fighting that infernal blush.

"Well, it is." He touched her cheek with his fingertips.

Her throat was as parched as if she'd walked in the desert for a week straight.

Grandpa Roger's voice intruded on the moment. "Can a third party join you? Or would I be in the way?"

Of course. Joe had said those things for her grandfather's benefit. Not hers. Why couldn't she seem to remember that?

Joe pulled back his hand. "Come on in, sir. Alicia's fixing breakfast."

"Wasn't what it looked like from here," her grandfather said, grinning at them like the Cheshire cat.

"How would you like your Egg Beaters, Grandpa?"

"Scrambled is fine."

"Joe? Eggs over medium?"

"No, you can scramble mine, too." He walked over to a drawer at the far end of the counter, opened it and moved some items around. "Where's the Phillips screwdriver, Alicia?"

"Something broken?" Grandpa Roger asked.

Not yet, but I'm afraid my heart's about to be.

The ski resort was packed on this first Saturday after Thanksgiving. Snow had come early to these westernmost slopes of the Rockies, and the skiers were out in full force.

While waiting in line at the lift, Joe heard some-one say it was the best opening in years. He looked forward to getting to the top of the mountain so he could experience it for himself. He needed something to clear his head. He hadn't been thinking like himself. Not since the day he'd met Alicia in that coffee shop.

He was almost starting to feel as though they were a family, he and Alicia and her grandfather.

A family. What did he know about being part of a family? An *Ozzie and Harriet* kind of family, that is. Dysfunctional he had no problem understanding.

As the lift swung around and picked him up, he muttered a few choice words beneath his breath. He was feeling too much and working too little. That's all that was wrong with him. Come Monday, he had to make serious changes in his routine. It was up to Alicia to entertain her grandfather during his visit. Let her take some time off work. She was the boss, Christmas season or not. She could jolly well spend time with the old man. Joe wasn't going to do it anymore.

A short while later, he skied off the lift. When he was out of the way of other disembarking ski-ers, he stopped to adjust his goggles and check his equipment, then he attacked the mountain with a vengeance, hoping to work off the last of his—

The last of his what?

Frustrations?

Irrational expectations?

Attraction to Alicia?

Whatever it was, he wasn't successful. Thoughts of Alicia and her grandfather went down the slopes with him. At the bottom he *whooshed* to a stop, pushed the goggles up onto his forehead and glared back in the direction he'd come, feeling out of sorts with the world.

A child began to wail, drawing his gaze toward the bunny hill. There they were, a group of mogul monsters, taking their ski class. The kid who was crying was probably no more than five years old. Maybe six. While Joe watched, a man strode onto the scene and knelt in the snow in front of the boy. His dad, apparently. The man talked to the kid, dried his tears, smiled reassuringly, and in what seemed no time at all, the boy was back with his class, grinning from ear to ear. The man looked on with parental pride.

Would I make a good dad?

The question nearly knocked him off his skis. There was no way that he wanted to have kids. Not a chance. Never.

He envisioned Alicia, her hands resting on her enlarged stomach, looking feminine, tender, beautiful.

Oh, no. It wasn't going to happen. No *way!*

He needed another run at the mountain. Maybe another dozen runs.

* * *

"You really like your new laptop, don't you, Grandpa?" Alicia looked over her grandfather's shoulder at the screen.

"I sure do. I've always used one of the retirement center's computers. They're old and clunky in comparison to this laptop. The clunky ones don't make me want to stay on very long."

"High-speed internet connection makes a difference, too. Do they have that in the center?"

"Yes, but yours seems faster." He turned his chair around. "Hope that husband of yours is having a good time."

That husband of mine...

"I like him, Alicia. I think you found yourself a fine man. I just wish I'd been at the wedding."

"Me, too," she answered softly while returning her gaze to the screen. "What are you looking up now?"

"Believe it or not, I've already managed to connect with two friends of mine from the ministry. Men I haven't talked to in years. We were in school together a lifetime ago."

"That's wonderful, Grandpa. If you know where to look, you can find just about anything you want on the internet, I guess."

"Mmm." Her grandfather shook his head, and his voice was grim. "Both good and evil, I'm afraid." He twisted on his chair, then laid a hand on Alicia's stomach. "You protect this little one, my girl. The world is full of traps."

She smiled, but her vision was blurred. "I will, Grandpa. I promise. I'll always take good care of Humphrey."

"Humphrey?" He chuckled as he patted her belly. "I hope you have a better name in mind for my first great-grandchild than Humphrey Palermo."

Palermo? Her heart did another one of those silly little flutters as she pictured Joe holding a tiny baby in his arms.

"So?" Grandpa Roger prompted.

She pulled herself back to the present. "I'm sorry. What were you asking?"

"What names have you chosen for the baby?"

"I'm not...*we're* not sure yet. We've still got time, so there hasn't been any rush to decide."

"No favorites at all?"

She shrugged. "I rather like Alexander for a boy and Jennifer for a girl."

"And what about Joe?"

She couldn't tell her grandfather she'd never asked her husband's opinion about baby names. So she told another lie: "He can't decide." She shrugged a second time. "You know how some men are. He says he's leaving it up to me to choose."

Her grandfather continued to look at her without saying a word, his gaze thoughtful.

"You know," she said taking a step backward, "I

think I'd better call the shop and see how the day is going."

With that, she turned and beat a hasty retreat to the kitchen where she picked up the telephone handset and held it to her ear.

For months she'd tested first names with her last name. Alexander Harris or Jennifer Harris. She'd liked the sound of those two the best.

But how would they sound with Palermo?

She pictured Joe again, holding a baby, smiling, crooning softly.

Alexander Palermo…

Jennifer Palermo…

"I've *got* to stop this." She hung up the phone without dialing. "It could never happen. It couldn't happen in a million years."

"What couldn't happen?" she heard Joe ask.

Her heart fluttered as she turned toward the door to the utility room. "I didn't hear you come in."

"That's because you were talking to yourself." He smiled, then asked again, "What couldn't happen?"

She shook her head. "Oh, just something from work. Nothing important."

Lying was getting to be a way of life, it seemed. Lying to her grandfather. Lying to Joe. Lying to herself. Why had she allowed lies to take over her life? She'd always been an honest person.

She drew a breath and asked, "How was the skiing?"

In his stocking feet, Joe stepped into the kitchen,

closing the utility-room door behind him. "Beautiful. You should've been there."

She wouldn't have thought it possible, but he appeared even more handsome than usual in his silver-gray ski pants and white turtleneck sweater. His cheeks were ruddy from the cold, and his spiky black hair looked damp. She was sorely tempted to run her fingers through it, try to restore it to order.

Instead she turned her back toward him. "It sounds like you had a good time."

"Yeah. And I plan to go up again soon."

"You should. It's why you moved back to Idaho, after all." Her heart hurt, making it difficult to speak.

"Alicia?"

She heard the soft fall of his stocking feet as he crossed the kitchen.

"Come Monday I've got to spend more time talking to local law firms." He lowered his voice to just above a whisper. "And I should find an apartment, put down a deposit to hold it. I'll need to be ready to move come the first of the year."

She nodded, still without looking at him.

"It'll be here before we know it."

"Time flies," she answered.

Out of the corner of her eye, she saw him lean his backside against the kitchen counter and cross his arms over his chest. "Where's your grandfather?"

"On his laptop." She had to meet his gaze now. "You created a monster."

Joe grinned.

It took her breath away.

She was falling for Joe Palermo. Falling fast and hard.

Big mistake. That's what had happened with Grant. She'd fallen fast and hard for him, and look where it got her. Divorced, pregnant and lying to her grandfather.

Joe watched the confusion swirling in her eyes and wondered what was going on behind them. He wished he could say something that would make her laugh, something that would make her eyes sparkle again.

But he knew better than that. He'd spent the day on the mountain trying to drive her from his thoughts. He'd almost succeeded.

Almost.

He cleared his throat as he stepped away from her, putting some distance between him and temptation. "I think I'll take a shower."

On his way through the living room, he paused long enough to greet Grandpa Roger, then headed for the bathroom. A short while later he stood beneath a hot spray of water, leaning his forehead against the glass door of the shower stall.

"I'm losing it."

Joe had never been and never would be some knight in shining armor riding in to rescue the damsel in distress. He was the dragon about to roast said damsel with flames from his nostrils. Like his father before him, he was an aggressive type A personality, a driven, self-motivated, self-obsessed kind of guy.

Not that God hadn't been working on him in those areas. He recognized that being self-obsessed wasn't an admirable trait. He even thought there'd been some headway made.

Still, a workaholic wasn't great husband or father material. If he cared for a woman, the least he could do was not allow her to think he might fill the spousal bill.

Temporary insanity was the only explanation for him being in this house, playing this role, and the sooner he got out of here, the better off he would be. Maybe he should try to convince Alicia to come clean to the old man. In lieu of that, he meant to bury himself in his work until he was rid of all these crazy thoughts.

Joe finished his shower, then donned a black T-shirt and a pair of Levi's. While in Alicia's bedroom, he decided to look once more for his missing driving glove. He knelt on the floor to look under the dresser when he heard the telltale growl of the enemy. He turned to see Rosie, crouched not far from his bare feet, her tail flicking from side to side. He scooted on his knees into the corner. Rosie released another of those feline, throaty growls, the kind that made his blood run cold.

He was trapped. Trapped by an enemy that couldn't weigh even ten pounds, but trapped all the same. He stood there, pondering his options.

There weren't many. In fact, as far as he could tell, there was only one.

He closed his eyes, clenched his jaw and breathed in deeply through his nose. "Alicia!"

He opened his eyes and looked at Rosie. He would have sworn she grinned, even while she threatened him with another throaty growl.

"Alicia!"

This had to be the single most humiliating moment of his life.

"Alicia, come here!"

"Joe?" The bedroom door opened, and Alicia stepped inside. "What is it?"

He glared at her, not feeling the need to explain.

When she figured it out, she tried not to smile but lost the battle. At least she didn't laugh out loud.

Thanks for nothing.

"I'm sorry, Joe." She hurried across the room and lifted the cat into her arms. "I don't know what's gotten into her. She really is a sweet-natured cat."

"Yeah, right."

"Bad, kitty," she whispered.

Well, he could chalk up one more reason he should play his part and then get out of here. He and this cat were definitely not suitable as roommates.

Alicia couldn't help grinning every time she thought of Joe—tall and strong man that he was— cornered by little Rosie. She'd learned in the past week that he had a fun sense of humor, but not when it came to her cat. And maybe the dog, too.

When they sat down for supper that evening, she could tell he was still a bit irritated, although he tried to hide it. It surprised her that she could read his mood so easily.

"I made some interesting discoveries while you were out today." Grandpa Roger spooned mashed potatoes onto his plate. "If you have time this evening, I do have a few questions I'd like to ask you."

"Sure. Be glad to." Joe's tone belied the genial nature of his words.

Grandpa Roger raised an eyebrow in Alicia's direction.

She gave him a slight shake of her head, as if to say: *Don't ask.*

He nodded, then said, "Joe, Alicia tells me you two haven't agreed on a name for the baby yet."

Joe's gaze lifted from the serving bowl of green beans that he held in his hand.

She smiled, not knowing what else to do or say.

"Naming your baby is an important decision," her grandfather continued. "The father should definitely participate."

Alicia wasn't feeling quite as amused as she'd been before.

"I remember when Alicia's grandmother was pregnant with Justin. Teresa and I spent hours poring over lists of names. It was a special time for the

two of us. Drew us even closer together than we'd
been before."

She looked down at her plate. Her appetite had
vanished along with her laughter.

"I'd only been home from my stint in the army a
couple of months when Teresa discovered she was
expecting. After the things I saw in Korea, her pregnancy seemed to be God's reaffirmation of life and
goodness. Those months were a joyous time for us
both." Grandpa Roger was silent a moment, then
added, "But I don't have to tell you two that."

"No, sir."

A lump formed in Alicia's throat, her amusement over Joe and Rosie replaced by sadness over
the things she would miss as a single parent. She
wouldn't spend time going over lists of names with
a husband. She wouldn't look back when she was the
age of her grandfather and remember the joy of ex-
periencing her pregnancy with the most important
person in her life. Even if she married again one day,
she wouldn't have the memories from now.

And it hurt. Hurt more than she wanted to admit.

"'Course, we hoped Alicia's father would be the
first of several children, but that wasn't to be. Teresa was never able to carry another baby to term."
Grandpa Roger took a few sips of water. "I hope
you'll be blessed with a full quiver."

"Sir?"

"From Psalms. 'Like arrows in the hand of a warrior, so are the children of one's youth. How blessed is the man whose quiver is full of them.'"

Alicia's gaze was irresistibly drawn to Joe. She was surprised to find him looking at her, his expression inscrutable. She had no idea what he thought or felt.

Her grandfather continued, warming to his subject. "There's a special glow about a woman who's with child. A special beauty. When my wife was expecting, I used to sit in a chair in the living room, right out there, and watch her as she did her sewing or knitting or whatever other busywork she did in the evenings. All I could think was how beautiful she was. Just like Alicia is now."

She glanced at her grandfather. "I'm far from beautiful."

He chuckled as he shook his head. "You're wrong, my dear. Ask your husband if you don't believe me."

It took everything within her not to burst into tears. Sadness did not begin to define the ache she felt in her chest. She would love to look at Joe and have him tell her she was beautiful, and he probably would. After all, he had a role to play in this charade. But he wouldn't mean it.

From somewhere deep within, she garnered the strength to smile at Grandpa Roger. "Those who love me might think me beautiful, but I feel more like the proverbial bull in a china shop." She slid her chair back from the table. "One that needs to be excused for a minute." She hurried from the kitchen, escaping to the sanctuary of her bedroom.

Ask your husband, her grandfather had said.

She moved to stand in front of the full-length mirror. She smoothed her maternity top over her stomach, and then turned sideways for a second look.

Perhaps a husband would think her beautiful. But not Joe, not the man who had found his way into her heart before she'd known what was happening.

Chapter Eight

Early on Sunday morning, Joe realized that he and
Alicia hadn't discussed the matter of church atten-
dance. Wouldn't her Christian friends notice if she
suddenly produced a husband? It wouldn't serve her
purposes if they said something in front of her grandfather. But as it turned out, he was worried for nothing. Alicia didn't have a church home.

"I didn't attend for a number of years," she said
over the monitor when he asked her about it. "I'm not
sure how that happened. My family was always in
church when I was a kid. Sunday mornings. Wednesday nights."

"I remember." Joe's own family never gave reli-
gion any thought. He'd been led to Christ by a friend
in college.

"After my marriage and divorce, I realized I
needed to get my life back in order, and that included getting right with God." She sighed. "But it

isn't as easy as I thought it would be, finding a place to belong."

"So where are we going this morning?"

"Grandpa's choosing."

"He knows you don't belong to a church?"

"Yes, he asked me about it yesterday when you were up skiing."

God willing, Alicia's search for a fellowship would help Joe find a place to worship in the Boise area, too. He pictured the three of them—him, a very pregnant Alicia, and her retired pastor grandfather—sitting side by side in a pew and wondered what the Lord thought of their masquerade. Was telling a lie ever right in God's eyes, even when it was done for a good reason?

Joe succeeded in keeping himself busy in the days that followed. He was less successful at keeping Alicia out of his thoughts.

On Sunday afternoon, after they had returned from church, Joe had gone to the slopes at Bogus Basin. On Monday, he'd gone to the library, ostensibly to do research, although he caught himself daydreaming all too frequently, and most of those daydreams included Alicia. On Tuesday he'd not only had interviews with two Boise law firms but he'd also checked out four apartments in different parts of the city. On Wednesday he'd spent long hours in the basement of Alicia's home, closing more of his files, preparing to ship them back to his old firm in California.

He'd spent as little time as possible with Alicia and Grandpa Roger, pretending it was the demands of work and not because he wanted to avoid them. He wasn't sure if he'd fooled the older man or not; he *was* certain he hadn't fooled Alicia.

He awakened on Thursday morning to the sound of a storm buffeting the old farmhouse. Naked tree limbs whipped the siding and scraped the windows and rooftop. He sat up, listening to the lonely wail of the wind.

After a moment, he got out of bed to look out the window and promptly stubbed his toe on a leg of the crib. He groaned but managed to swallow a few choice words as he sank onto the bed again.

"Joe?"

When would he remember she could hear him all the time through that stupid monitor?

"Are you all right?"

"I'm fine. Just ran into something in the dark." He picked up the monitor, bringing it closer to his lips. "Don't you ever sleep?"

"The storm woke me."

"Me, too."

"There must be ten inches of snow on the ground."

"Really?" He rose to have a look for himself.

"The valley almost never gets that much snow."

The back porch light revealed a winter wonderland beyond the window.

"You going in to work today?" he asked.

"Not today."

"Good. The roads will be bad. You shouldn't be driving in this."

They were silent awhile.

"Joe?"

"Yeah?" He sat down again.

"I need to ask a favor."

Another one? "What?"

"Grandpa asked if he can visit my birthing class that starts soon. He wants to go with us."

"Us?"

"Yes." Her reply was nearly inaudible. "Just once, he said."

"Ooh, boy."

"I'm sorry, Joe."

He raked the fingers of both hands through his hair. "I guess it can't be helped. Not unless you decide to tell him the truth. Which I still think you should do."

She hiccuped.

At least, that's what he thought he heard. But a moment or two later he realized she was crying. "I didn't mean to make you cry."

Over another choked sob, she answered, "It isn't your fault. It's my own. I got myself into this mess."

"True enough." He smoothed his hand over his hair. "But with good intentions."

"I'm sorry," she repeated. "I never realized how hard this would be on you."

"I'm a big boy. I can take it."

"Even Lamaze?" There was a note of amusement in her voice now.

"Even that," he answered, not sure that he spoke the truth.

"You're a special kind of man, Joe Palermo."

Her words caused threads of emotion to wrap around his heart, confusing him. He should get out of this mess and fast. But he couldn't leave her, couldn't disappoint her, couldn't break his promise. Why? Some misplaced sense of obligation?

Who was he kidding? He couldn't leave because he wanted to be here—here with Alicia.

Alicia was surprised to find she'd drifted back to sleep. It was the sound of a snow shovel scraping concrete that awakened her the second time.

Feeling groggy and out of sorts, she got up and walked to the window, slipping into her robe as she went. She pulled back the curtains—and was blinded by the brightness of the snowy morning.

Wearing his ski garb, Joe shoveled the back walk. He worked with a steady, smooth rhythm, sliding the shovel beneath the heavy snow, then effortlessly raising it over his shoulder and letting the snow fly toward the yard.

It was nice to have a man around the house.

She groaned as she turned from the window. How corny could she get? What was she going to do next? Start wearing a shirtwaist dress, heels and pearls

while she did the housework? She'd been shoveling her own sidewalks for eleven winters, ever since
she inherited this house from her grandparents. She
could have shoveled them today, too, even big, fat
and pregnant. She wasn't helpless.

Humphrey gave her a stiff jab in the ribs.

"Ouch!" She looked down and touched her stomach. "Well, I could. And exercise would do you good,
too, little one."

Scrape...scrape...scrape... The sound drew her
gaze back to the window.

"It *is* nice to have his help."

More than nice...wonderful.

More than wonderful...because it was Joe.

She touched the windowpane with the palm of
her hand. "How could I let this happen?" she whispered. "How could I let myself begin to love you?"

A knock sounded on her door. "Alicia?" her
grandfather said softly from the hallway.

"Yes?"

"May I come in?"

"Yes."

Grandpa Roger wasn't smiling when he stepped
into the room.

"Morning, Grandpa."

"Alicia, did you and Joe have a disagreement?"

She shook her head, wondering what prompted
the question.

"I don't mean to pry, but I saw him coming out

of the nursery this morning. It looked to me as if he'd slept there."

Oh, dear. Now what did she do?

"You don't have to tell me if you'd rather not. I just thought—"

"Nothing's wrong, Grandpa." She turned toward the window, hiding her face from her grandfather's shrewd eyes. "We didn't fight. I was restless in the night. Lots of tossing and turning. When I get like that, sometimes Joe goes into the other room so he can get some sleep. It actually helps me because then I'm not uncomfortable *and* regretting that I'm keeping him up, too."

"I see."

"You don't have to worry about us. We're fine."

There was a lengthy silence.

Then her grandfather said, "All right, my dear."

A moment later the bedroom door closed and she was once again alone.

Scrape...scrape...scrape...

"Oh, Joe I wish..."

But she didn't dare speak her wish aloud. It would only make her heartbreak more complete when January came and Joe was gone from her life.

Much as Alicia had been doing when he entered her bedroom a short while before, Roger stood at the kitchen window and watched Joe shoveling snow off the walk between the back porch and the unattached garage.

Roger Harris hadn't served fifty-five years in the ministry without learning a thing or two about people. His granddaughter was lying to him; she was as transparent as glass. Things weren't right between her and Joe. It was obvious Alicia loved that young man, and Roger believed her husband returned her love. But sometimes, the way they acted, the way they spoke, it all seemed so…so…

He shook his head, wishing he could put his finger on what bothered him. More important, he wished he could put his finger on what bothered them.

Christ told His followers that knowing the truth would set them free, but He was speaking of Himself. Jesus was the Truth, and it was knowing Him that set people free. Not all truth accomplished freedom. Some truths could keep a person in bondage for years without the grace of God.

Still, Roger would like to hear the truth from these two young folks. He would like to understand what was going on in this home. If he knew what was amiss, perhaps he could help Joe and Alicia find their way.

He closed his eyes and took his concerns to his Father.

After two decades in California, Joe had forgotten what hard work shoveling snow was. But it had served a good purpose. He'd worked off a lot of his frustration by the time he finished.

As he stepped through the back door into the utility room, he smelled breakfast cooking. Bacon, if he wasn't mistaken.

"Another month here, and my cholesterol's going to be off the charts."

He removed his boots and set them on a rug next to the door. Then he hung his coat on a hook, sticking his gloves in the coat's pockets. He hesitated before taking his first step toward the kitchen door. He wanted to make certain Rosie wasn't lying in wait for him.

Man, how he hated that cat.

The coast appeared clear, so he proceeded toward the kitchen. But it wasn't Alicia whom Joe discovered standing at the counter, removing a golden-brown waffle from the waffle iron. It was Grandpa Roger.

"Hungry?" the older man asked. "I figured you must've worked up quite an appetite, clearing all the walks."

"I could eat." Joe glanced toward the living room. "Where's Alicia?"

"In the shower, I think."

If circumstances were different—if Alicia weren't carrying another man's baby, if she weren't the type of woman who wanted husband, home, family—he would have welcomed a relationship with her. He liked being with her.

When she wasn't crying.

As if reading his mind, Grandpa Roger said, "Pregnant women aren't always easy to live with."

"What?"

"I said, pregnant women aren't always easy to live with." He carried a platter of waffles and bacon to the kitchen table.

"Is *any* woman?"

Grandpa Roger chuckled. "You have a point." He motioned for Joe to sit down. "Alicia said she wasn't hungry yet, so we'll go ahead without her."

After Joe had sat down, the older man blessed the food, then passed the platter across the table.

"The bacon is all yours." Grandpa Roger sighed, a sound of true regret, but he quickly changed the subject back to Alicia. "My wife was like Alicia when she was expecting our son. I never knew what would upset her. Seemed I was always making an egregious error of one kind or another. If she wasn't crying, then she wasn't speaking to me."

Joe nodded.

"And during those last months of her pregnancy, I hardly got a single good night's sleep. My, how Teresa tossed and turned. Sometimes she even talked in her sleep. Alicia ever do that?"

"Not that I've heard. But then, I'm a sound sleeper. I can sleep through almost anything."

Grandpa Roger looked thoughtful. "Lucky you."

Joe had the strange feeling he'd said something wrong, although what it could be, he hadn't a clue.

The older man filled his juice glass, then took a few sips. Afterward, he set the glass on the table, his right index finger tapping the rim. "Love covers a multitude of sins."

"Sir?"

"I was reflecting on forgiveness. Without the ability to forgive, my marriage to Teresa never would have lasted fifty-three years."

"Fifty-three years?" Joe let out a soft whistle. "That's a long time."

Grandpa Roger smiled. "Yes. And worth every bit of effort to make it last, too." He took another sip of juice. "What about your parents? How long have they been married?"

"They divorced while I was in law school. Mom's remarried now. Dad's come close a few times to taking another plunge, but he hasn't gone through with it. I don't think he will. He's soured on marriage." He almost added, *Like father, like son*.

"That's a shame."

Joe shrugged. "Yes, but my folks were miserable when they were together."

Rags trotted into the kitchen, nails clicking on the linoleum, interrupting whatever the older man might have said next. Right behind the dog came Alicia, her hair still damp from the shower. She wore a hot-pink maternity top with big black polka dots on it, a pair of black leggings, and those silly bunny slippers.

She looked adorable.

Made Joe wish he could get up and give her a real kiss.

"Good morning." She stopped behind her grandfather's chair. "Thanks for making breakfast." She kissed him on the top of his head. Then her eyes shifted to Joe. "You had a busy morning."

"Yeah."

"The walks look great."

"Had to be done. Gotta be able to get to the cars."

She went to her chair and sat down.

"Are you ready for a waffle?" Grandpa Roger asked as he lifted the platter.

"No. Just juice, thanks."

Joe passed her the carton. "Are you feeling all right?"

"I'm fine." She didn't look at him.

"Don't forget you're supposed to be eating for two."

She glanced up and their gazes met.

After a moment he smiled at her. A few seconds more and he realized it was important that she smile at him in return. More important than it should have been *if* he hoped to avoid further emotional entanglements.

Which he did.

Didn't he?

Chapter Nine

The following Saturday was another hectic day at Bundles of Joy. Only three weeks before Christmas, the shopping madness was in full swing.

Alicia had hired several seasonal salesclerks, but there still didn't seem to be enough help. There never seemed to be a moment for anybody to sit down and rest their aching feet, let alone for Alicia to take her customary catnap.

It was nearly four o'clock when she finished ringing up a customer who was outfitting an entire nursery for her son and his wife.

"It's the least I can do for my first grandchild, don't you think? I'd nearly given up on them having children."

As the woman left the store, Alicia noticed Joe standing near the shop doorway, watching her. She had no idea how long he'd been there. She glanced around, looking for her grandfather, but he was nowhere to be seen. She felt a spark of alarm.

"Where's Grandpa?"

"I left him napping in front of the TV."

"Is he feeling all right? He isn't—?"

"He's fine. You need to quit worrying."

"I just thought…when I saw you alone—"

"Can't a man come to take his wife out to dinner, if he wants?"

Her heart skipped a beat.

"Even if she's a make-believe wife?" he finished with a conspiratorial wink.

Disappointment flooded through her.

"Your grandfather considered it a good idea."

"Be honest. It was his idea to start with. *He* put you up to this, didn't he?"

Joe gave her a wry smile. "He's a hard man to argue with. I'm learning I might as well just go with the flow."

She nodded in agreement. "I won't be finished here until six."

"That's okay. I don't mind waiting. I'll do some Christmas shopping and come back for you."

Who would he be shopping for? Alicia wondered.

As if she'd spoken the question aloud, he said, "What is it you want for Christmas?"

"Me? But you don't have to buy me a—"

"Yes, I do. What would your grandfather think if I didn't give you a gift for our first Christmas together?"

She sighed. "I guess you're right. I suppose you'd better tell me what you want to find under the tree, too. A wife should know these things."

"Surprise me." His grin broadened, and his gaze seemed to caress her cheek. "I love surprises."

"Do you?" she asked, feeling breathless again.

He leaned closer, lowered his voice. "Yes, as a matter of fact, I do. Don't you?"

"I'm not sure."

She'd been surprised by her feelings for Joe Palermo; she loved him more than she'd thought possible. But did she like that surprise? No, not when she suspected how much it was going to hurt later on.

Downtown Boise was aglow with Christmas lights. Store windows were draped with garlands of green, the glass sprayed with frosty-white images of elves and bells and pine trees, the displays enticing. The chilly December wind hadn't kept shoppers at home. Even this late in the afternoon, the sidewalks and department stores and small specialty shops were filled with men, women and children in search of the perfect gifts for their loved ones.

Stopped outside a dress shop, Joe turned up his coat collar and stared at a pretty party dress of aquamarine chiffon in the center of the window display. The color matched Alicia's eyes. It would look great on her—in a couple more months.

He shook his head. He didn't want to give her something she couldn't use now.

He turned and continued down the sidewalk.

Alicia hadn't told him what he should get her for Christmas. Not even a clue. She wouldn't need anything for the baby. She could buy those things wholesale. Besides, he wanted his gift to be just for her. Something personal. Something for Alicia alone.

What did a man buy for a wife who was still a stranger to him?

He stopped at the corner and waited for the light to change, giving him permission to cross the street. A squeal of joy caused him to turn and look behind him. A couple—no more than twenty years old, either of them—stood in front of a jewelry store display, kissing each other, mindless of the staring passersby.

Young love. At first it seemed his thoughts mocked them, but after a moment he realized it was envy he felt, not disdain.

The light changed and the crowd surged around him, but Joe didn't move. He watched the couple go into the jewelry store. He couldn't seem to help himself. He followed them.

Inside the store, he observed the couple as they leaned over a display case filled with wedding and engagement rings.

"Pick the one you like best," the young man said.

"No, I want the one *you* like best."

They kissed again, their eyes open, as if they couldn't get enough of the sight of each other.

A salesclerk arrived at Joe's side. "May I help you find something, sir?"

"No, I—" He stopped himself and changed his answer. "Yes. I'd like something special…for my wife." He glanced at the clerk's name tag. Bridget, it read.

"Do you have anything in mind?" she asked.

"I'm afraid not." He shrugged. "I'm not every good at this sort of thing."

"How much did you want to spend?"

He shook his head, then shrugged again.

"Why don't you step this way? We have a nice selection of earrings. Does your wife have pierced ears?"

He had to think for a moment. "Yes."

"Perhaps she would like some diamond earrings." She smiled at him. "I've never known a woman who could have too many diamonds."

That statement would have fit his ex-wife, he thought as he followed Bridget, and it would have fit some of the women he'd dated over the years since his divorce.

But Alicia?

He imagined her in that oversize pink bathrobe and wearing those silly bunny slippers. He grinned. For some reason, diamonds didn't fit the picture.

"Not diamonds," he said to himself as he veered away from Bridget.

He found what he hadn't even known he was seeking in the display case farthest from the store's entrance. A ring with two small pearls and a cut stone the same blue-green as the dress he'd seen earlier. The same blue-green as Alicia's eyes. The ring was dainty, understated. Perfect for Alicia Harris.

"Did you find something?" Bridget asked when she caught up to him.

"There." He placed his index finger on the glass. "That ring there."

"Oh, that's a lovely choice. Let me get it out for you." She leaned down to unlock the back of the case. "What size ring does your wife wear?"

"I'm afraid I don't know. Her hands seem small to me."

Bridget raised her eyebrows, and Joe suspected it took great effort for her not to roll her eyes, too.

"Let me see your hand." When she held it up, he continued, "Looks to me like about the same size. Try it on."

She placed it on the third finger of her right hand. It fit perfectly.

"I'll take it."

Alicia's back was killing her and so were her feet.

"Sit down and rest," Susie ordered in a motherly tone. "I'm capable of closing the till without your help."

Alicia decided not to argue; she sank onto a nearby stool that was tucked behind the counter.

Her assistant manager glared at her. "You need to take time off until after the baby comes."

"I'm fine. The doctor doesn't think I need to stop work until—"

"I don't care what *he* thinks. Look at you. You're exhausted."

"But this is our most important time of the year."

Susie straightened, tilting her chin upward in defiance. "Are you saying I can't be trusted to manage the store, Ms. Harris?"

"Of course not." Alicia released a deep sigh.

"Then stay home and enjoy your grandfather. He came all the way from Arizona to be with you, and his health isn't the best. You don't know how many more opportunities you'll have to be with him."

"That's true."

A rap on the locked door drew both of their gazes. There was Joe, motioning to be let in.

"Stay home and enjoy *him,*" Susie added.

Without comment, Alicia pushed up from the stool and walked—actually, it was more of a waddle—toward the entrance. She turned the dead bolt, then pulled the glass door toward her, allowing him in, along with a blast of frigid air.

"You ready to go?" he asked.

Alicia glanced at Susie. "I'm ready." She wouldn't have dared say anything else. "I'll get my coat."

"No. Stay here. I'll get it for you. You look beat."

His comment made her feel fat and frumpy. He hadn't meant it that way, but that was the effect, nonetheless. Maybe it would be better if they went straight home and forgot going out to eat. It was her grandfather's idea, anyway, not Joe's. He wouldn't mind. He would probably be glad if she changed their plans.

When Joe returned with Alicia's coat, Susie said, "You make sure she eats a good supper. She's been working way too hard."

"I'll make sure," he answered.

"I told Alicia she ought to go on maternity leave now, but she won't hear of it. See if you can talk some sense into her."

Joe looked at Alicia, one eyebrow slightly raised. "I'll try."

She sighed.

"Ready?" He held up her coat.

"I'm ready." She turned around and slipped her arms into the sleeves.

"Then let's go. I'm starved." He took hold of her arm, then glanced over his shoulder. "Night, Susie."

"Good night, you two. I'll lock the door behind you. Have a good time."

Joe's grip on Alicia's arm tightened as they stepped outside into the wind. "My car's in the parking garage across the street." He steered her toward the crosswalk. "I thought we'd go to Malloy's. Is that okay?"

"Fine with me."

It wasn't far from downtown to the restaurant on Broadway Avenue, but heavy traffic made it seem farther. It was a good thirty minutes before they pulled into the parking lot at Malloy's Seafood Bar and Grill. They had to park in back.

"Looks as if we might have a wait," Joe said when he opened the passenger door for her.

"As long as there's a place to sit down."

He took her arm again. She liked the feel of it.

Maybe this wasn't such a bad idea…even if she did "look beat."

Joe, on the other hand, looked marvelous. Alicia was aware of the women in the restaurant who stopped what they were doing in order to stare at him.

Hands off, ladies. He's mine.

But he wasn't hers, and the futility of her situation cut through her like a knife through the heart.

"We're in luck," Joe said after speaking to the maître d'. "They can seat us now. Come on."

Their table was in a small alcove, giving the illusion of private dining. Alicia was grateful for that. She needed some isolation from crowds and noise.

Joe helped her off with her coat, then pulled out the chair for her. She mumbled her thanks as she sat down.

The waiter handed them each a menu while telling them that evening's specials. "I'll be back to take your order," he said before walking away.

While Joe perused the menu, Alicia watched him, wondering how she had allowed herself to care for him this way. Why hadn't she guarded her heart? Grandpa Roger would tell her that no mistake is wasted if a person learns from it. Why hadn't she learned her lesson when it came to falling in love in a rush?

This man, as wonderful and kind as he was, didn't want marriage and a family. Given her advanced pregnancy, it was obvious she would be all wrong for him. In a matter of weeks, she would be a package of two. If a man loved her, he would have to love her child, as well.

She lowered her gaze to the menu in her hand.

God, please remove these feelings from my heart. I don't think I have the strength to have it broken again. Not with Joe.

After a few failed attempts to jump-start a conversation, Joe decided to allow Alicia to eat her supper in peace. Not that she did much of a job of it. It seemed to him that she spent more time moving food around on her plate than consuming it.

He was about to ask what was troubling her when she whispered, *"Oh!"* Her hands went to her abdomen.

Joe's gaze followed hers, and he was amazed to see her maternity top move, as if driven by a wave beneath the surface. "What was that?"

"The baby."

It happened again.

"The baby?"

She looked at him, smiling. "I get tired, and Humphrey gets active. Happens all the time."

"I've never seen that before."

She was silent a moment, then asked, "Would you like to feel it for yourself?"

"I don't know…"

"It's okay if you do. I don't mind."

"Are you sure?"

She took hold of his hand, placing it on her belly. "I'm sure."

He waited…and waited…and waited. He was about to withdraw his hand when he felt something. Something strong and almost sharp.

He looked up, meeting her gaze. "What *is* that?"

"Most likely a knee or an elbow. Could be a heel."

"And this happens often?"

She laughed. "Often enough."

"Does it hurt?"

"No. Not usually, anyway."

He drew back his hand. "Amazing."

Amazing, indeed. Something inside Joe stirred as surely as the baby had stirred inside of Alicia. This was a life. This was a miracle. As the psalm said, God Himself had knit this child together in his mother's womb. This precious life was wonderfully complex. God had seen this baby before he— or she—was conceived and had already recorded every day of little Humphrey's life long before now.

Did all expectant fathers realize how amazing it was, this small creation, this new life? No. Not all of them. Humphrey's father hadn't. But now Joe had, and he wasn't any too sure what to do with that discovery.

"Joe?"

He met her gaze.

"Grandpa's worried about our marriage. He thinks we're in trouble."

"Why's that?"

"He knows you were sleeping in the nursery. He saw you coming out of that bedroom the other morning. I...I told him another lie. I said you slept in there when I was too restless." She looked out the window. "I thought it would be easier than it is."

"What would be easier?"

"Pretending we're married."

He wanted to comfort her but wasn't sure how. "We haven't done too bad of a job, all things considered."

Her voice dropped to a near whisper. "But we don't act like two people in love."

He remembered the young couple in the jewelry store, the way they'd gazed into the other's eyes with... adoration. Had a woman ever looked at him that way? Had he ever felt that same depth of devotion?

"It can't be easy for you to act the part." She looked at him again. "I'm not very attractive these days."

He leaned forward. "You're wrong, Alicia. You look beautiful."

"I wasn't fishing for compliments." The smile that curved the corners of her mouth had a hint of wistfulness about it.

"I wasn't serving up a compliment. I meant it."

But he could see in her eyes that she didn't believe him, and before he could think what to do or say next, their server arrived with the check. The moment to say more—to say things he didn't yet understand—was gone. A short while later, they left the restaurant, words still unspoken, emotions swallowed up in silence.

Chapter Ten

Joe didn't sleep well that night. He heard every creak the old house made. Making matters worse, that button on the monitor in Alicia's room was stuck again. He heard every breath she took, every whimper out of Rags, even Rosie as she padded around on one of her nocturnal inspections.

That would have all been bad enough if he'd understood *why* he couldn't sleep, if he could pinpoint the reason and then deal with it. But it wasn't that simple. This had more to do with fuzzy impressions and disturbing, unnamed emotions than with anything concrete.

Joe dealt better with the concrete than with the abstract. Probably what made him a good lawyer.

He had just checked the clock for the umpteenth time—7:00 a.m.—when he heard Alicia's gasp. A sound of pain.

"Alicia?" He whispered into the monitor. "What's wrong?"

"Nothing." The word was barely out of her mouth when she caught her breath again.

He picked up the monitor. "What is it?"

"Just a stitch in my side. That's all."

"Are you sure?"

"I'm sure. I'm all right."

"You don't sound all right."

"Well, I am."

He spoke in his sternest lawyer's voice. "I think Susie's right. You need to stop working until after the baby comes."

"Don't be ridiculous."

"*I'm* not the one being ridiculous. I'm telling you, you need to stay home."

"And who do you think you are to tell me what to do?"

Joe switched on the bedside lamp. "I'm the one with the common sense."

Alicia didn't reply right away. When she did, her anger was unmistakable. "My work schedule is *none* of your business." She enunciated each word with care.

"It is as long as we're playing this little charade of yours," he replied with the same precision. "Your grandfather would expect it. Remember? I'm supposed to be your husband. Even a guy like me knows you need to rest and take better care of yourself. At least think about the welfare of the baby."

"How dare you?" she whispered.

"I dare plenty when I care enough."

Alicia didn't reply to that.

He'd said more than he should have. "You're single and over twenty-one. Do what you please." He set the monitor on the nightstand, rose and dressed, then headed for his basement office.

Before he reached the stairs, his outrage had evaporated. Alicia was right. It wasn't any of his business. She could decide what was best for herself.

He should apologize to her. He was out of line and he knew it.

Once in his office, he booted up his laptop, listening as it whirred to life, making all its usual sounds before it was ready for his first command. He considered opening his word-processing program and doing a bit of work, but he logged on to the internet instead, hoping a visit to one of his favorite sites would take his mind off of Alicia.

He looked over the snow reports for Bogus Basin, Brundage Mountain and Sun Valley. He priced new skis, boots and poles. He even checked on a two-week vacation package to a resort in Switzerland.

Alicia remained all the while in his thoughts.

He wasn't sure what possessed him to go to a search engine and enter the word *maternity* in the search box. The first links in the list of websites didn't improve his spirits: complications of birth, difficult births, breech delivery.

Then he found some options on birthing classes. Curious, he followed the links and began reading.

By the time he heard footsteps on the stairs, he had a passing knowledge about the Lamaze and Bradley natural childbirth methods, understood about birthing rooms and "mother-friendly" hospitals and had printed off a copy of Ten Tips for a Healthy Pregnancy as well as several pages of frequently asked questions.

He closed his internet browser just as Grandpa Roger appeared in the doorway.

"Am I intruding?" the older man asked.

"No. Not at all. I was about ready to go upstairs and get myself something to eat."

"Mind waiting a minute or two?"

Joe shook his head. "No, sir."

Alicia's grandfather settled onto a wooden chair that had seen better days; it rocked slightly on its uneven legs. The elderly man's expression was grim. Apprehension tightened Joe's belly.

"You know," Grandpa Roger began, "I've come to like you in the short while I've been here."

"Thank you, sir. The feeling's mutual."

"You and Alicia seem right for each other."

Uh-oh.

Grandpa Roger's eyes narrowed as he looked across the desk at Joe. "Society's mores have changed a great deal during my lifetime. Not always for the better. In some circles nowadays, marriage is considered passé. Even among some who call themselves

Christian." He gave his head a slow shake. "I'm not part of those circles, Joe. I remain firmly convinced that men and women should wed before they are physically intimate, and I most definitely believe they should be legally joined in matrimony before they bring children into the world." He leaned forward. "Do you think those beliefs are antiquated, young man?"

"Ah…no, sir."

"Good. Then will you tell me why you haven't married my granddaughter?"

Joe glanced toward the stairway, then back at the older man.

"I overheard you two talking this morning. From separate rooms, I might add. I put two and two together and got four. You've arranged some elaborate hoax for my benefit."

"Sir, I—"

"Do you love her?"

"Yes. Yes, of course I do." Was that a lie or the truth?

"And you want to participate in raising your child, give him a good home?"

It wasn't his child but his answer came swift and strong. "Yes."

"Then I expect you to do right by them both. I expect you and Alicia to get married. If you love her and want to be a part of her life and your baby's life, then there's no reason you shouldn't."

"Mr. Harris…sir…well, you see, the reason we haven't—"

"Don't tell me." The dread on the older man's face might have been comical if it hadn't made him look as if he were about to suffer another heart attack. "You're not a married man, are you?"

"No, sir, I'm not married. I was once, ten years ago. I never planned to go through that again."

Grandpa Roger visibly relaxed. "I see. Once burned, twice shy. Is that it?"

Joe nodded. It was true, after all.

"Children?"

"No." Joe rose from his chair. He would have paced the office, only there wasn't enough room. "I think I should talk to Alicia."

"That was my thought, too."

"I'll go now."

Grandpa Roger stood. "We'll go together."

"But, sir, I—"

"You'll find I'm a stubborn old man, Joe, when I choose to be. This is one of the times I choose to be."

Alicia stared at her reflection in the mirror over the sink. There were dark circles under her eyes, and her complexion was pallid.

Maybe Joe and Susie were right.

She winced, hating to admit that, even if only to herself.

"I *am* tired. Terribly tired."

She hoped her grandfather would understand

when she told him she wasn't going to church this morning. She didn't have the energy.

She sighed. She owed Joe an apology. He'd been concerned for her welfare. Maybe he'd overstepped his bounds a little, but their argument was her fault. She'd been out of sorts and had made him pay for it.

She turned from the sink and left the bathroom. No point putting it off. She would make her apologies now.

Joe and her grandfather were standing in the middle of the living room when Alicia emerged from the hallway. Something in Joe's expression caused her to stop in her tracks.

"We need to talk," Grandpa Roger said.

Joe gave an almost imperceptible shake of his head, followed by an equally subtle shrug.

"Let's all sit down," her grandfather added. "Shall we?"

Apprehensive, Alicia sat in the wing chair closest to the piano. Joe sat across the room from her in the recliner. Grandpa Roger settled onto the couch.

"Alicia, my dear girl, I overheard your argument with Joe this morning," her grandfather began. "Your door was ajar."

Her heart sank. She lowered her gaze to a spot on the hardwood floor, about three feet in front of her.

"I can only surmise why you have concocted this pretense. I suspect it was to protect me. For my health."

She nodded.

"I won't judge you, Alicia, for the choices you've made. It isn't my place to sit in judgment. But I'd be in error if I didn't encourage you to do what your heart knows is right. I've witnessed the love you and Joe have for each other. Your baby should have the privilege of seeing it, too."

"Oh, Grandpa," she whispered.

He continued, his voice gentle but firm. "Whatever impediment you perceived that kept you from marrying before now, it can be overcome. And I hope, if the impediment was my reaction when you called me last spring, that you can forgive me for my careless words."

She looked up, knowing the moment had come to tell the truth. The whole truth. "Grandpa, I think you should know that—"

"Your grandfather's right," Joe interrupted, rising to his feet. "We should get married." He stepped toward her, skirting the coffee table. "I told him about my being divorced and never intending to marry again. But he's right. That's no excuse. We should do as he says."

"But, Joe, we can't—"

He knelt beside her chair. "We can work things through. I know we can." He took hold of her hands, pressing them together between his. His eyes beseeched her not to argue with him. "Marry me."

She could scarcely think over the din of her pounding heart.

"Say yes."

In some remote part of her brain, she knew this couldn't be happening, that she was dreaming and any moment now she would wake up.

"Say yes."

"Yes," she whispered.

Her grandfather stood. "You two should be alone."

She was aware of Grandpa Roger leaving the living room, heard the click of his bedroom door closing behind him, but her gaze never strayed from Joe. Not even for an instant. She wanted the fantasy to continue a little longer. She wanted to believe in the love her grandfather thought he saw. She wanted to pretend she was carrying Joe Palermo's baby and that he loved her and wanted to marry her, wanted them to be a family.

Joe shattered the romantic daydream with a few softly spoken words.

"Good thing you played along." He released her hands, then rose to his feet. "I think the shock might've killed him. You should've seen him down in the basement. I was really worried."

She blinked.

"I'll draft a prenup agreement that'll protect us both," he continued, just above a whisper. "The marriage can be annulled after your grandfather goes back to Arizona."

Her throat ached, and her chest hurt.

Joe leaned down, touched the back of her hand, forcing her to look at him once again. "It'll be okay. It's only for a few weeks. I can be convincing in my role as the new husband. I've come to care for your grandfather too much to let anything happen to him because of me."

He cared for her grandfather too much. But what about her? Had he made this offer because she meant something to him?

"He already thinks the baby is mine," Joe added, his words persuasive. "Let him think it awhile longer. Just until he's clear out of danger."

She drew a shaky breath. "He looked bad when you were in the basement?"

Joe nodded.

God, what should I do? Would this be wrong? Worse than the lies I've already told?

"We'll see this through, Alicia. We'll make sure your grandfather's okay."

Perhaps, but she couldn't help wondering if she would be okay when it was all over.

Chapter Eleven

Joe was as good as his word. His prenuptial agreement, which he presented to Alicia on Tuesday morning before she went to work, covered all the bases.

"I had another lawyer look it over," he assured her. "He's got plenty of expertise in domestic law. We don't want any unforeseen problems later on. It was his idea to add this." He pointed to a section of the document.

The clause specified that Alicia's baby was not Joe's offspring, and he would not now nor at any future time be expected to provide financial support for it.

The daddy clause, she thought sadly as she read it a second time. Or, to be more accurate, the *non-*daddy clause.

Suppressing a sigh, she signed the document and handed it back to Joe without comment. She would rather die than let him see how wounded she felt by it all. She was doing this for the sake of her grandfather, she kept telling herself. For her grandfather and no other reason.

But even for Grandpa Roger she wouldn't change her mind about where to have the wedding. They would be married by a judge at the county courthouse. Period. No argument. Her grandfather would be one witness, Susie Notter would be the other. No invitations. No announcements. No celebrations. Nice and simple.

"I'm eight months pregnant" was the only explanation she would give her grandfather for her decision. "I don't want a church wedding and all the fuss that goes with it. It would be rather inappropriate at this juncture, don't you think?"

Only to herself did she admit the real reason for her choice of a civil ceremony—because she couldn't bring herself to speak false vows in church. She couldn't pledge before a minister to remain with Joe "until death do you part" when the truth was they would part in a matter of weeks. This was what novels called a marriage of convenience. It wasn't meant to be real and lasting.

On Friday morning, five days after her grandfather had confronted them in her living room, Alicia, Joe and Grandpa Roger got into Joe's SUV and drove to Boise. It was snowing again, and it took twice as long as normal to reach the courthouse. Susie was waiting for them by the main doors.

"Judge Smith's in court now," a woman behind

the counter told them while checking her wristwatch. "But he can marry you during his next break. About another half hour, I'd guess." She motioned to an empty bench. "Have a seat, and I'll call you when he's free."

"Thank you, miss," Grandpa Roger said.

Joe cupped Alicia's elbow with his hand and guided her to the bench. "Can I get you anything while we wait?"

She shook her head, reminding herself that he was playing his part—the solicitous bridegroom.

"Well, I'm thirsty." He glanced down the corridor, first to the left, then to the right. "I'll be over at the water fountain." He pointed.

"I'm going with him," her grandfather said.

"It wouldn't hurt you to smile a little," Susie whispered in her ear. "It's your wedding day."

Smile? Alicia couldn't remember how. "What am I *doing* here?"

"What you think you need to do." Susie took hold of her hand and gave it a comforting squeeze.

Alicia looked toward the water fountain.

Grandpa Roger *seemed* well enough. She'd seen no signs of ill health this week, no indications his heart was acting up. He walked more slowly than he used to; he slept later in the mornings and took a few naps during the day. But didn't most people his age slow down and sleep more? Joe had said Grandpa Roger looked ghastly on Sunday morning when the two of them talked alone. That being the case, she

must be doing the right thing, for her grandfather looked healthy this morning.

"What I need to do," she said, repeating the words like a mantra.

"There aren't many guys who would agree to this. Joe must care about you a lot."

"He's very kind."

As if realizing they were talking about him, Joe turned his head and met Alicia's gaze. He smiled and winked at her.

She forgot to breathe.

"Ow!" Susie protested. "Let up."

Alicia looked at her friend.

"You're breaking my hand."

She glanced down. "I'm sorry." She released her grip. "I didn't—" She stopped, not knowing what she'd intended to say. She lifted her gaze, tears welling in her eyes, blurring her vision. "Oh, Susie."

"Oh, no! You *love* him!"

Alicia shook her head in denial, at the same time closing her eyes.

"Yes, you do."

This time she nodded.

"Look at me," Susie commanded.

Reluctantly Alicia obeyed.

"Does Joe know how you feel?"

"No."

"You should tell him."

"I can't."

"But—"

"He doesn't want marriage, Susie, and he doesn't want kids. I want both of those things. I want them a lot. Joe and I don't have a future together, so it wouldn't serve any purpose for him to know how I feel."

Susie shook her head.

"I'll get over it," Alicia whispered.

"Will you?"

"I'll have to." She released a sigh. "What choice do I have?"

Joe hadn't imagined he would ever again repeat wedding vows to anyone. But there he was, standing before Judge Smith in chambers, promising to be a husband to Alicia Harris. He knew it was in name only and temporary besides, but he felt as though it was real, all the same.

What surprised him was that it felt real…and he didn't seem to mind.

In fact, he felt good.

Maybe that had something to do with the woman at his side. She looked lovely in her ivory-colored maternity dress with its long sleeves and delicate lace collar. He couldn't imagine any bride looking prettier. Still, he wondered if she minded not having all the usual bride's trappings—white gown of satin, lace and pearls, a bridal veil, a church full of flowers and friends. She deserved all of those things.

"Do you have rings to exchange?" the judge asked, interrupting Joe's thoughts.

"Yes."

Alicia glanced up, clearly surprised by his answer.

He removed the ring—the one he'd planned to give her for Christmas—from his pocket. "I hope it fits," he said softly.

She watched as he slipped it onto the ring finger of her left hand. Then she looked at him again.

"It matches your eyes," he added, feeling an explanation of some sort was necessary.

"It's beautiful. But I didn't get a ring for you."

He answered her with a smile.

In less than two minutes more, the judge pronounced them husband and wife. Joe gave Alicia a kiss, keeping it brief and dignified. Afterward, all parties signed the license as required by law, Joe paid the judge his fee, and it was over.

Beaming with joy, Grandpa Roger hugged Alicia, then Joe. "I'm so pleased…. This is wonderful…. God bless you both…."

When Susie embraced Joe, she whispered, "You take good care of her. You hear me?"

"I hear you." He was bemused by the pointed look she gave him when she stepped back. It was as if she were trying to tell him something more, but he had no idea what it might be.

"I'm taking everyone out to eat," Grandpa Roger announced. "My treat."

"That isn't necessary, Grandpa."

Joe took hold of Alicia's arm. "Yes, it is." He

leaned in close to her ear. "He wants to do it. Let's let him."

She replied with a nod, but he sensed her continued reluctance.

The four of them—Grandpa Roger, Susie and the newlyweds—left the judge's chambers and walked toward the main entrance of the courthouse.

"You'll come to eat with us, won't you, Miss Notter?" Grandpa Roger asked.

"Can't. Gotta get to the shop. My boss is a tough cookie." Susie grinned as she glanced over her shoulder at Alicia. "Right?"

"Right," Alicia replied with a smile of her own.

But Joe noticed the smile never reached her eyes, and that bothered him. He wanted her to be happy today.

He wanted her to be as happy as he was.

The truth hit him like a pro boxer's punch to the solar plexus. He nearly stumbled over his own feet in his surprise.

Happy? To be married?

Okay, so he knew it was temporary. That could explain it. Their marriage was as much pretend now as it had been before a few words were spoken and a piece of paper signed.

Still…Joe Palermo, happy to be married?

Impossible!

Alicia was miserable.

What had she done to deserve this? Married twice

in one year and neither of them destined to last more than a few weeks. Was she so unlovable?

It was ridiculous to think such things, she argued with herself. This had nothing to do with whether or not a man could love her.

But neither of her husbands had loved her.

That wasn't fair to Joe. She shouldn't compare the two men or the two marriages. Grant had used her, but Joe had done her a favor. Joe cared enough about both her and her grandfather to carry on this pretense for Grandpa's sake. He was kind and generous and thoughtful and…and she loved him.

Which brought her back to *why* she was miserable.

Seated next to Joe in the half-empty restaurant, Alicia cast a furtive glance in his direction.

My husband.

Something warm and torturously sweet coiled in her belly. At the same time, pain pierced her heart.

Oh. Humphrey. I wish Joe was going to be your daddy.

Tears blinded her.

"Excuse me," she whispered as she slid from the booth. "I'm going to the restroom." She hurried away before either man could see her tears.

In the ladies' room, Alicia leaned her back against the locked door and let them fall. She'd been holding it in all week, but now she let her pent-up hurt and frustration and loneliness and fear and anger come sobbing out. She cried because she was married and still alone. She cried because she wanted what she couldn't have. She cried because she'd believed in happily ever after, and didn't want to stop believing.

When the storm had finally passed, she stepped to the sink and stared at her reflection in the mirror. Her eyes were bloodshot, her eyelids puffy, her nose red. Black streaks of mascara ran down her cheeks.

"The beautiful bride," she whispered as she turned on the water and moistened a paper towel.

When she married Grant, she'd been blissfully, ignorantly happy. Infatuated by his charisma. In love with being in love. She hadn't known she'd married a jerk who would be cheating on her before the ink on the license was dry. Grant had never been kind to her. Not like Joe.

She met her gaze in the mirror again.

Not kind like Joe...

She looked down at the ring on her hand, at the blue-green stone and pearls. It was a beautiful ring, a costly one if she knew anything about jewelry. But it was the gesture behind the ring that meant the most to her.

It hadn't occurred to her to buy a ring for him. Not knowing, as she did, the way he felt. A ring would have proclaimed to the world that he was a married man, and that was something he didn't want to be.

"It matches your eyes."

The memory of his words, of the way he'd looked at her as he slipped the ring on her finger, caused a fluttering sensation in her stomach.

Would a man who felt nothing for his bride have

noticed that the stone was the same color as her eyes? Wasn't there a chance—even just a glimmer of a chance—that Joe acted out of more than mere kindness? Wasn't there a chance it was more than concern for her grandfather that caused him to marry her instead of letting her tell the truth?

Hope came surging back. Perhaps without reason. Perhaps without wisdom. But there it was—hope.

"I've got three weeks," she told her reflection. "Three weeks before Grandpa leaves. I'm not going to waste them feeling sorry for myself."

Joe was beginning to worry. Alicia had been in the ladies' room a long time. Maybe he should check on her. She'd looked kind of pale when she left the table. Maybe she was sick. Or maybe she'd passed out. Women did that sometimes when they were pregnant; he'd read that the other day when he was on the internet. Maybe she was lying unconscious on the bathroom floor.

Those thoughts had no more occurred to him than he saw Alicia weaving her way toward their table. Relief spread through him. Their gazes met as she drew near. She smiled, and for the first time today, her smile appeared genuine.

"You okay?" he asked.

"I'm fine." She slid into the booth beside him. "Sorry I took so long." Her gaze remained locked with his.

She had the most amazing eyes. Like the ocean

found in warm climes like Hawaii and the Caribbean, like those beaches and coves where people went snorkeling. He had the absurd feeling that if he could dive into her eyes, like a snorkeler into the ocean, he would find beautiful surprises beneath the surface, surprises more precious than pearls and coral and bright-colored fish.

Joe felt heat rise up his neck. He'd never been given to romantic notions. He'd never understood poetry that compared a woman to a summer's day. He was the practical sort, logical and levelheaded in all circumstances. Or at least, he used to be.

"Have you ordered?" Alicia asked.

"We were waiting for you." He was thankful he sounded halfway normal.

"I'm starved." She looked at her grandfather. "I guess my case of nerves is over."

Funny. Joe was just beginning to feel nervous.

"Drop me off at the Senior Center on your way home," Grandpa Roger said as Joe drove his vehicle out of the restaurant parking lot an hour later. "You two should have this day to yourselves."

Alicia liked the idea.

"Are you sure, sir? There's not likely to be many people at the center with these roads as slick as they are. We didn't have anything special planned for this afternoon."

"I'm sure. It's your wedding day. Spend it together, just the two of you." He tapped Joe on the shoulder. "Drop me off at the center. I'll get a ride home."

"Sir, I really don't—"

"Don't argue with your new grandfather, my boy."

Alicia turned her gaze out the passenger window. Snow continued to fall in huge wet flakes, blanketing everything in white.

Pristine, clean, fresh, new. If only she could have come to Joe as such a bride. Not that she would wish away Humphrey. She wanted her baby. She loved him. Or her. But still she couldn't help wishing…

She felt Joe's hand close over hers where it rested on the center console. Despite herself, she looked his way.

"Your grandfather's right," he said softly. "Every bride deserves to do something special on her wedding day. What would you like to do?"

I'd like you to hold me and kiss me and tell me you love me.

"Alicia?"

"Let's just go home."

"Okay." He glanced over his shoulder, then back at the road. "We'll plan a honeymoon for after the baby arrives, Grandpa Roger."

Oh, how she hoped that would turn out to be true.

They left Alicia's grandfather at the Senior Center as he'd requested. The rest of the drive was made in silence. Once at the house, Joe parked the SUV as close to the back door as he could get. Then he hur-

ried around to the passenger door and helped Alicia
to the ground. He took a firm hold of her arm with
his left hand while he slipped his right arm around
her back. He didn't want her falling and hurting herself or the baby.

Was this the way all husbands felt toward their
expectant wives?

They reached the back porch door without mishap.
Joe opened it, then let Alicia go in ahead of him. He
caught up with her before she reached the door into
the utility room.

Even if Joe had been grilled for hours by the fin-
est attorney in the country, he couldn't have found an
answer for what happened next. He was as surprised
as Alicia when he swept her feet off the floor and,
cradling her in his arms, carried her into the kitchen.

"Joe, what are you doing?"

"I'm carrying my bride across the threshold.
That's what."

"Well, put me down. I'm too heavy."

"You're not too heavy," he said, even as he obeyed
her command.

She didn't move away as he'd expected. Instead,
she tipped her head and looked up at him, her gaze
filled with a woman's unfathomable secrets.

He was the one to take a step backward. "I suppose it was a crazy thing to do."

"Joe…" She reached out, touched his chest with
the tip of her fingers. "I…I want you to know how

much I appreciate your friendship. You've done so much for me and Grandpa."

Was her gratitude what he wanted?

"But you don't have to pretend our marriage is real when Grandpa isn't around. I don't expect you to. Let's just continue to be friends. Let's not allow this charade to get in the way of that."

There was wisdom in her words. So why was he disappointed by them?

Chapter Twelve

Alone in the house for the first time in five days, Joe stood in the center of the nursery, his left arm resting on the top step of the ladder. Spread around him on the floor were a bucket, several double-roll bolts of prepasted wallpaper, a can of paste, two brushes, a sponge, a wall scraper, a razor knife, a straightedge and two rollers. On the table next to him were a pencil, tape measure, chalk line, level and pair of scissors. In his hand he held a booklet the clerk at the paint and wall-covering store had told him to read before he got started.

He grinned, thinking how surprised Alicia would be when she got home. Just yesterday she'd told her grandfather that she'd meant to paper the nursery months ago but never got around to it. Now, she'd said, it would have to wait until after the baby came because she was too big and awkward to do the work.

Her comment had been followed by a deep sigh that had said volumes more than her words.

Joe didn't want her to have to wait. The nursery should be just what she wanted now, not later. It seemed to him Alicia had to put off too many things. He'd like to see her happy. Really and truly happy.

His grin faded, replaced by a frown.

Something had changed between them in the days since they spoke their marriage vows before the judge—something beyond his moving into her bedroom. Of course, that wasn't much of a change. He had taken up residence on the small sofa in the far corner of the bedroom, and he always had a reason to stay up at least thirty minutes after she went to bed, thus giving her time to change into her sleepwear and get under the covers. Legally married they might be, but she still deserved her privacy, given their plans to end the marriage in due course.

Hopefully they would do a better job of hiding their revised sleeping arrangements from her grandfather than they had managed to do with their original arrangement.

He smiled now as he remembered the way she looked when she exited the bedroom in the mornings, clad in her pink robe and slippers, her short hair disheveled, a sleepy smile tipping the corners of her mouth.

How did she manage to look happy first thing in the morning?

There was something about Alicia, something

about being with her that made him want to stay. If a real marriage could be the same as this temporary one, he wouldn't think of leaving.

He looked forward to listening as she and her grandfather talked about her girlhood. He liked hearing her laughter, a sound that invaded the deepest corners of his heart. There were times when he looked at her—times when she placed her hands on her round stomach and tipped her head to the side and smiled that secret smile, looking as if someone had whispered something wonderful in her ear—that he thought her the most beautiful woman in the world.

He gave his head a slight shake. "You think too much, Palermo. Just get to work."

He glanced at the booklet in his hand, then tossed it aside unread. How hard could it be to hang wallpaper? He'd asked the clerk plenty of questions while picking up the supplies. He didn't need this, too.

He grabbed the level and pencil off the table. Alicia had said she would be home between four and four-thirty. That didn't give him much time to finish his surprise.

Alicia was reaching for a stuffed toy on a top shelf when a sharp pain shot through her. With a gasp she doubled over, cradling her abdomen with her arms.

"Alicia!" Susie's hand alighted on her back. "What is it?"

She drew a few slow breaths before she attempted to straighten.

"Alicia?"

She shook her head. "Nothing," she finally managed to answer. "Just one of those twinges I get every now and then."

Susie looked at her customer. "Let me get someone else to assist you." She called to Judy to help the woman find what she wanted, then she took hold of Alicia's arm and said, "Come with me."

Alicia was propelled by Susie's firm grasp toward the back room. Once there, with the door closed behind them, Susie made Alicia sit down. Then she stood guard over her with arms crossed in front of her chest.

"I'm all right, Susie. You can leave me to rest a moment. I won't need long."

"No."

"Really. I—"

"Alicia, you're putting on your coat, and I'm taking you home, and you aren't coming back until your baby is at least six weeks old."

"Susie—"

"I mean it. If you don't cooperate, I'll tell your grandfather the truth about you divorce from your baby's father *and* I'll tell Joe you're in love with him."

Alicia stared at her friend.

"You think I won't do it, but you're dead wrong. I *will* do it if you don't do exactly what I'm telling you now. I know Bundles of Joy's procedures as well as you do. I can balance the tills and manage the checkbook, and I'm better at hiring and firing than you ever were—except when you hired me, of course." She punctuated her last comment with a saucy grin.

"But it's almost Christmas."

"So?"

"So we're shorthanded as it is."

Susie's expression turned serious again. "The store is having its best Christmas season ever. You can afford to hire a couple more people. And I'll work every day if I have to. It isn't worth the risk for you to stay."

It was Susie's last words that made up Alicia's mind for her. Besides, she *was* tired, and those sharp, unexpected pains *did* alarm her.

"You win," she said softly.

"About time."

"But I can get home without you chauffeuring me."

"Are you sure? The roads are still slick in spots."

Alicia nodded, then pushed herself up from the chair. "I'm sure. I drove myself to work. I can drive myself home."

"Well…okay. But you call me when you get there."

"I will." She gave her friend a hug. "Thanks, Susie."

"No prob. You take care of yourself. And make sure that husband of yours does his part."

She turned toward the coatrack. "Joe's always helpful." She suppressed a sigh. "You can rest easy. I'm in good hands."

Joe had measured and cut, according to the advice the clerk gave him, but he hadn't taken into consideration that he would need to match the pattern, too.

Hanging wallpaper was more difficult than he'd anticipated.

He looked at the pile of wet, soggy, discarded paper. He'd pulled a strip off the wall moments before. If he kept this up, he would run out of paper before the room was finished. Not a good thing, according to the clerk at the paint store.

Maybe he should look at those instructions, see what else he might be doing wrong. A glance at his watch told him he didn't have time to *find* the booklet, let alone read up on the fine art of hanging wallcovering. He needed to hurry if he was going to finish before Alicia got home.

He laid the new strip of paper on the table, then moistened the back side with the paint roller before slapping on some wallpaper paste with a brush. As he carried the paper to the stepladder, he noticed the drops of paste on the hardwood floor.

"I hope this stuff cleans up okay."

Getting up the ladder while keeping control of the sticky wallpaper wasn't easy, but he made it without too much trouble. His skills seemed to be improving by small increments.

It would've helped matters if this old farmhouse had walls that were plumb. Matching both the paper pattern and getting a straight alignment were not easy tasks. And the paste didn't seem to want to adhere the way he thought it should.

Again he wondered about that instruction booklet.

He muttered a few words beneath his breath as he tried to smooth wrinkles out of the paper, working his way from ceiling to floor. He had just knelt on the floor and was reaching for the utility knife when something cold fell on his head and back.

"Not again."

The paper had come off the wall and landed on him in one big, gooey mess. He pushed it off, but the paste remained in his hair, on his clothes, smeared across his arms and even one side of his face.

That's how Alicia found him.

She couldn't help herself. She burst out laughing.

Joe stopped trying to wipe off the paste with his fingers and swiveled toward the door. The expression of mixed surprise and disgust on his face only made his predicament seem all the more amusing.

"It's not *that* funny," he said as he got to his feet.

Alicia nodded, covering her mouth with her hand, trying to hide her smile. "Yes, it is."

"Only because it didn't fall on you."

A renewed fit of giggles kept her from replying.

"I was trying to do you a favor." He kicked away

the paper that was stuck to his shoe, then took a step toward her. "Have you no appreciation?"

He wasn't really angry, was he?

But even that threat wasn't enough to stifle her laughter. If he could see himself, he would laugh, too.

"I warned you."

Before she could react, he was across the room. He grabbed her with his paste-covered arms and pulled her close. Then he kissed her.

If what he'd meant to do was silence her laughter, his methods worked.

Alicia's mind went blank. There was only the feel of his arms, only the taste of his mouth, only that uniquely masculine scent that was Joe's alone. Her arms snaked around his neck. She wondered if he could hear the riotous pounding of her heart.

I love you, Joe. I love you. I love you. I love you.

He cradled her face between the palms of his hands before drawing back slightly. Their gazes met and held.

"What're you doing home so early?" he asked, his voice almost gruff.

"I'm officially on maternity leave." She forced a smile. "Susie wasn't taking no for an answer."

"Good for her. It's what I said ten days ago. Remember?"

She wished he would kiss her again. Instead, he removed his hands from her face and took a step back. She had no chance but to let him move out of her arms.

"I'm sorry I laughed," she said, forcing herself not to step forward, not to seek his nearness again.

He shrugged, and a wry grin curved the corners of his mouth. "I must have looked pretty funny, at that."

She smiled. "Yes, you did. You still do."

"I thought it'd be easy." He grabbed a sponge from the worktable, then reached out and wiped paste from one of her cheeks. "Sorry. Didn't mean to share the mess."

"It'll wash off."

He turned his back toward her, looking at the partially papered wall. "I wanted to have it done before you got home."

"It was sweet of you. Really. I mean it."

"It needed to get done." He glanced over his shoulder, a twinkle in his eyes, his brows raised. "I should've read the instructions."

"I love you, Joe." She hadn't planned to tell him, but she shouldn't have been surprised when she did. The feelings—her love, her joy, her hopes, her dreams—had become too big to hold in any longer.

Her joy was short-lived.

The look on his face said it all.

A heavy silence filled the room; it pressed upon her chest, threatening to crush her, body and spirit. She would have given anything to be able to unsay the words.

He turned fully toward her. "Alicia..."

"No." She stopped him with a raised hand. "Don't. Let's pretend I didn't say that." She faked a laugh.

"Can we blame it on my pregnancy hormones? I blame them for everything else."

He continued as if she hadn't spoken. "You know I care for you, Alicia, and I'm sure you care for me. We're friends, like you've said before. But I'm not good husband material."

Here came those tears. She blinked, trying valiantly to keep them from falling.

"Alicia, I—"

She laid her fingertips against his lips. "I know. You're right. We're too different. We want different things." She pulled back her hand. "It would be the height of stupidity to believe we could make a marriage work."

"Well, maybe not *that* bad."

She knew he was trying to lighten the mood with his teasing.

It didn't work.

"Maybe you should leave," she whispered. "Maybe it's time to tell Grandpa the truth about us and put an end to this sham."

Logically, Joe knew she was right. It was time for him to go, for them to stop playing house. It was time to tell the truth.

Yet, everything inside him rebelled against it.

They stood there, in the middle of the nursery amidst the disarray of his disastrous wallpapering attempts, their gazes locked. He could see his own confused emotions mirrored in her eyes, and he wished he could wipe it away for both their sakes. If he could find the right words…

But before he could try, the sound of the back door slamming shut intruded.

Alicia turned away from him. "That'll be Grandpa." She left the nursery, her back straight, her head held high.

She's going to tell him now.

Alarm shot through Joe, and he followed her as she headed for the kitchen. He didn't know what he intended to do or say. He only knew he wanted to stop whatever was about to happen.

But what happened wasn't what he'd expected.

"Grandpa!" Alicia cried.

Joe stopped in the kitchen doorway, taking in the scene before him. Grandpa Roger had collapsed on one of the vinyl chairs. His arms hung loose at his sides while his head rested on the table surface. His eyes were closed. He looked unconscious.

"Grandpa?" Alicia touched his shoulder.

He groaned in response.

"Joe, call for an ambulance."

He was already headed for the phone.

"Wait." Her grandfather sat up slowly. "I don't need an ambulance." His words were whispery thin.

Joe held the receiver in his hand; he could hear the drone of the dial tone. "Are you sure?"

"I'm sure. Just help me to my room. I only need a short rest."

"But Grandpa…"

Her grandfather took hold of her hand. "Relax, my girl. It's not a heart attack. I'm overtired. That's all."

Alicia glanced toward Joe, her eyes filled with fear.

Joe figured it wasn't wise to argue with him. Better to do as he said and call the doctor later.

He placed the receiver in its cradle, then crossed to the table. "Ready?" He put one arm around the elderly man's back.

"I'm ready."

"Okay. Here we go." With care, he helped Alicia's grandfather stand. "We'll go only as fast as you want, sir. You set the pace."

Grandpa Roger nodded. "Sounds good." He glanced over his shoulder. "Would you get me a glass of water, my dear? I'll want to take one of my pills."

"Right away." Her voice quavered.

"Do what you can to comfort her," Grandpa Roger said softly as he and Joe left the room. "I don't want her making herself sick over me."

"You worry about yourself. I'll take care of Alicia."

"I know you will. And it does my heart good to see the way you love her. Does my heart good."

By the time Grandpa Roger was lying on his bed, covered with a handmade quilt, Joe had to admit he didn't look too sick. His coloring was good, and he seemed to be breathing normally. He hoped Alicia was coming to the same conclusion as she hovered near the bedside, watching her grandfather dutifully swallow his pill.

"I'll leave the door open, Grandpa," she told him. "You call if you need me."

"A nap is all I need, and I'll be fine." He waved his hand in a gesture of dismissal. "Now go on, both of you, and let me be."

Alicia obeyed with obvious reluctance.

As they stepped into the hallway, Joe thought she looked in far worse shape than her grandfather. From the telltale quiver of her chin, she was fighting tears.

"He's going to be fine." He drew her into his arms. "You'll see."

Alicia hid her face against his chest. "Oh, Joe, I was so scared."

"Your grandfather's okay." He kissed the top of her head. "We'll take him in to see the doctor if it'll make you feel better." He patted her back. "Don't worry, Alicia. Don't worry. He's going to be fine."

Hearing his granddaughter tell her new husband that he should leave and put an end to "the sham," as she'd called their marriage, had made Roger Harris's head hurt. No doubt about it. Still, he may have laid it on a little thick, using his health against them in his attempt to force those two to work things through instead of giving up.

Why was it that he could see so clearly the love they felt for each other and neither of them could see it?

Lord God. He closed his eyes. *Draw Alicia and Joe closer to You so that they might also grow closer as man and wife. Help them find their way. Grant me wisdom so that I may guide and not hinder.*

He thought of his wife and wished she were still living. Teresa would have known exactly the right thing to do. She'd been blessed with the gift of discernment, and her compassionate heart had helped her use that gift for the benefit of everyone whose lives she touched.

Roger had to work a little harder at finding God's will. Knowing that, he reached for his well-worn Bible on the nightstand.

I love you...

In the wee hours before dawn, Joe stared at the ceiling and let the memory of Alicia's words play over and over again in his head.

I love you, Joe.

Was it possible she really loved him? That she wasn't merely grateful for his help? And if it was love she felt, what did she want from him in return?

He suppressed a groan.

He might not know the answers to the first two questions, but he knew the answer to that last one. She would want marriage. She'd want the real thing.

He'd been inches from a clean getaway. She'd told him to leave, that they were going to end the charade once and for all. If not for her grandfather's weak spell that afternoon, Joe would've been out of there. Gone. Vanished from her life.

Wasn't that what he wanted? Freedom.

He wasn't husband material. His faults were legion, too many for any woman to want to overlook. His failed first marriage had proven that. God had been working on him, helping him change, but there was a long way to go for him to become the man the Lord wanted him to be. Besides, didn't one of the epistles say it was better to be single?

As for kids? Well, if he was bad husband material, he would be even worse father material.

I love you, Joe.

Why had he married her? Had it really been just to do her a favor?

He recalled the moment he'd kissed her in the nursery, smudging her cheek with wallpaper paste, and a question began to churn in his head: If he had a chance for something more in his life, if he had a chance to love and be loved, would he take it or let it slip away?

Chapter Thirteen

Pale morning light fell through the nursery windows. Long icicles, hanging from the eaves beyond
the glass, cast odd shadows across the hardwood
floor, a floor covered with ruined wallpaper. It was
rather emblematic of the mess she'd made of her life,
she thought as she stuffed another strip into a large
garbage bag.

She heard water running in the shower and knew
Joe was up. She released a deep sigh. They needed
to talk about what had happened yesterday, but she
wasn't sure she was ready yet.

Holding the garbage bag over her shoulder, she
left the nursery. She paused at the guest room door
and peeked inside. Her grandfather still slept. She
was thankful for that. She meant to make certain
he spent the day right there, except for a visit to the
doctor.

She continued her way to the kitchen where she

pressed the button on the coffeemaker to start it brewing. Then she carried the garbage bag through the utility room and deposited it on the back porch. Rags had completed her morning inspection of the yard by this time and dashed into the house while the door was open. Alicia paused long enough to ruffle the dog's ears before filling both food and water dishes. Those chores finished, she reentered the kitchen.

Joe was waiting for her there.

"You didn't have to clean up the nursery," he said as she closed the door behind her. "I would've done it."

She shrugged. "I didn't mind. I was awake."

"How's your grandfather this morning?"

"He's sleeping peacefully. But I'm going to ask him to see the doctor."

"Probably a good idea. It would make *you* feel better if nothing else."

"You're right about that."

He looked out the window.

She glanced down at Rags, standing next to her, tail wagging.

"Alicia—" Joe began.

"Joe—" she said at the same time, looking up again.

They both stopped, their gazes locked.

Finally he said, "You first."

"About yesterday."

"It's okay. You don't have to explain."

"You're wrong, Joe. I *do* need to explain. Or at least talk about it. We can't pretend it didn't happen."

For a moment she thought he might disagree.

But then he nodded. "Let me get my coffee first."

She breathed a silent sigh of relief as she sat at the table.

I wish I didn't love you, Joe. It would make everything so much easier.

Coffee mug in hand, he sat opposite her. He looked too handsome, too self-confident, too much like an attorney.

She lowered her gaze to her hands, clasped atop the table. "When I suggested you help me by pretending to be my husband, I never imagined things would get so complicated."

"I know that."

She gave her head a quick shake but didn't look up. "Don't interrupt, please. Let me get it all said."

"Okay."

"I was ready to tell Grandpa the truth. You know I was. But after yesterday's spell, I'm back to being afraid what the truth would do to him." Her hands clenched more tightly. "I can't take the risk. Not as long as I have a choice."

"I'm not asking you to risk it. I plan to see this through."

"I know you will." Now she looked up. "Because that's the sort of man you are."

He frowned a little, as if not sure what she meant.

"Joe, I'm not going to ask for more than you can

give. I shouldn't have said I loved you." Silently, she added, *I do love you, but I shouldn't have said it.*

He opened his mouth, then closed it without speaking.

She gave him a small smile of thanks. "What I'm asking is that we go back to behaving like friends again. We like each other. There's even some mutual attraction, I think." She had to look away, afraid he would deny it. "If not, we never would have married, not even for Grandpa's sake."

Above the rapid beating of her heart, she heard the tick of the clock on the wall and the soft *whir* of the refrigerator.

Shoring up her courage, she lifted her gaze to meet his. "It would make it so much easier during the next fifteen days if we remembered we were friends first. Then it won't be so hard to pretend we're anything more." She extended her hand toward him. "Fair enough? Friends?"

The clock continued ticking; the refrigerator kept whirring.

"Fair enough," he said at last, taking hold of her proffered hand. "Friends."

She wondered how it was possible to smile while her heart was breaking.

That evening Joe took hold of Alicia's arm and helped her out of the vehicle.

"Are you nervous?" he asked as they walked toward the medical clinic's entrance.

"I don't think so."

"Good thing one of us isn't."

She laughed, a pretty sound in the crystal cold night.

Joe was glad for it. He was glad for the talk they'd had, glad they'd cleared the air. He was glad she'd realized she wasn't in love with him, that they were good friends and nothing more.

Inside at the front desk, Alicia asked for directions to the birthing class.

"Right through that door and to your left. In the conference room. You can't miss it."

The woman was right. They couldn't miss it. Four other couples had arrived before them. The women were all well along in their pregnancies. One looked as if she must be carrying triplets, triplets who could make their entrance at any moment.

Joe didn't feel much like joking now.

An attractive woman in her thirties—the only one not obviously pregnant—approached Alicia and Joe with an outstretched hand and a welcoming smile. "Hello. You must be the Palermos." She shook Alicia's hand first, then Joe's. "I'm Pat Grisham, your instructor. We were just about to get started with a video." She motioned toward a grouping of chairs in front of a television set and, speaking to everyone in the room, said, "Please take your seats."

If anybody had told Joe two months before that he would find himself surrounded by pregnant women while watching a video of a live birth, he'd have told them they were insane. But there he sat. And the odd thing about it was, he found it fascinating. Okay, the video made him a little squeamish, but it was still fascinating.

He wondered what it would be like to be present in the delivery room, watching as his child was born.

When the tape ended, Pat Grisham turned off the television and faced the five couples. "So…are we ready for delivery?"

Nervous laughter swept through the group.

"I guess you know it's too late to back out now," the instructor said.

It wasn't too late for Joe. He wouldn't be around for the delivery of Alicia's baby. He wasn't the father.

He looked at the other couples, husbands and wives awaiting new additions to their families. One couple was young, no more than late teens or early twenties. Another couple looked to be in their forties. The other pairs were somewhere in between, more like Joe and Alicia.

Like Joe and Alicia.

Like a husband and wife.

Like a couple.

The Palermos.

Strange. That didn't sound bad.

For the most part, Alicia had been happier today. She was determined to love Joe and take pleasure in what they had now, this moment, and not to worry about tomorrow.

But when Ms. Grisham instructed each husband to reach around his wife and place his hands on her abdomen, Alicia was reminded how much she'd ached for his touch. Now that she had her wish, she wanted it to *mean* something, too. To *really* mean something.

"Humphrey's active tonight," Joe said softly near her ear.

The warmth of his breath on her skin caused gooseflesh to rise along one arm.

"It's an amazing thing, isn't it?" he continued.

"Awesome." She knew he was talking about the baby, but her heart meant something—or rather, someone—else.

"Dads," their instructor droned on, "don't be surprised if your wives say some rather...shall we say, *unkind* things to you during labor."

Despite herself, Alicia leaned the back of her head against Joe's shoulder and closed her eyes. It was easy to pretend he was her husband in his heart as well as legally, that he was the father of her baby. It was easy to imagine going home with him tonight and crawling into bed and snuggling close.

"Hey," Joe said, "what are you smiling about?"

"Nothing much." Without opening her eyes, she rolled her head from side to side. "Just thinking."

"Must be happy thoughts."

"Very," she whispered. "Very happy thoughts."

* * *

"How was your class?" Grandpa Roger asked them upon their return home.

Joe helped Alicia out of her coat. "It was fine."

"We watched a video of a baby being born." There was a teasing twinkle in her pretty eyes as she looked at him. "Joe turned green around the gills."

"I *what?*" he protested in mock indignation.

Her smile brightened. "It's true, and you know it." She turned to her grandfather, who was seated at the kitchen table, and gave him a kiss on the cheek. "I thought Joe was going to pass out. It was sad. Very sad."

"She's telling a whopper, sir. Don't believe a word of it." Joe leaned against the counter and crossed his arms over his chest. "The instructor warned the men about irrational behavior and unkind remarks. I see she was right."

Alicia laughed. "She meant *during* labor."

"Does that mean you're practicing being irrational and unkind?"

"I have not yet begun to fight." She punctuated the famous quote with a flourish of an invisible sword.

"Wish I'd felt up to visiting your class." Grandpa Roger rose from his chair. "But if there's going to be fainting and fighting, it's just as well I stayed home." He gave Alicia a return kiss on the cheek, then smiled at Joe. "A word to the wise, my boy. Accept the fact that the wife, especially when pregnant, is always right. It will make things much easier on you."

"Thanks, sir. I'll take your advice under consideration."

"Good night, you two."

"Good night," they answered in unison.

Once her grandfather had left the kitchen, Joe returned his gaze to Alicia. "Would you like a cup of tea?"

"That would be nice." She covered a yawn with the flat of her hand.

"Tired?"

She nodded.

"Why don't you get comfortable while I fix it for you?"

"Sounds wonderful. Thanks, Joe."

Alicia returned to the kitchen five minutes later, wearing her sweats and slippers. Rosie followed her mistress into the room. The cat stopped when she saw Joe near the stove, then she arched her back and hissed, announcing her displeasure.

He wondered if a hot teakettle, thrown from six feet away, could kill a cat. "Maybe I should find out."

"Find out what?"

He kept staring at Rosie. Only the cat's tail twitched; otherwise, she was motionless.

"Joe?"

Rosie darted out of the room, as if she'd guessed what he was contemplating.

Triumphant, Joe grinned. "Nothing important."

"Hmm."

The kettle's whistle rescued him from having to say more, and he was thankful for that. He didn't want to spoil the evening by saying—*again*—that he hated her cat.

He filled a mug with hot water, then carried it and the variety box of herbal teas to the table. "Here you go."

"Thanks."

He sat across from her and watched as she selected her tea bag, dropped it into the cup, and stirred until the color was right.

"You were a good sport tonight," she said softly.

"Good sport?"

She glanced up. "You know what I mean."

"Hey, I enjoyed myself."

An arched eyebrow proclaimed her skepticism.

"It's true."

She smiled and sipped her tea.

Why did it bother him so much that she didn't believe him? He couldn't say he blamed her. He'd made it clear he wasn't interested in kids and all the things that went with them.

And yet he hadn't minded a single minute of the class. Not even the video. He wasn't sure how to describe his feelings, except to say he'd felt a part of something important.

"Joe?" Alicia set her mug on the table. "Would you help me get a tree tomorrow? We need to make things more festive around here. For Grandpa's sake if for no other."

"Sure. Be glad to. There was an article in today's paper about a place to chop down your own tree."

He was about to tell her what else the article had said—about the horse-and-sleigh rides, the barbecued ribs and hot chocolate, and the carolers—but she spoke before he had the chance.

"*Chop?* I was thinking more along the lines of the tree lot near the center of town." She placed one hand on her belly. "I don't think I'm up to much more than that."

"Tell you what," he said, unwilling to give up on the Currier and Ives image in his head. "If I promise you won't have to chop anything, not even so much as an onion, will you go to the mountains with me? Just the two of us. We can ask someone to stay with your grandfather if it would ease your mind."

For several heartbeats, she said nothing. Then that soft, pleased smile of hers returned, gently curving the corners of her mouth.

"Okay, Joe, I'll go with you. If that's what you want."

Chapter Fourteen

Alicia awakened early the next morning, feeling as excited as a child. She'd dreamed about being in the mountains with Joe, watching him chop down tall trees. The dream had been so real she would have sworn she smelled the scent of pine in the room.

A whole day alone with Joe. It sounded wonderful.

But she didn't allow herself to read more into it than what was on the surface. She would savor every moment and be thankful for it. She would love him with all her heart. But she wouldn't ask more from him than what he freely offered.

Beside her, Rosie stirred, meowed, stretched, then climbed onto Alicia's lap—what there was of it. Seconds later Rags plopped her muzzle onto the mattress and whined.

"Morning, Rags," she whispered as she patted the dog's head.

The aroma of coffee drifted into the darkness of the bedroom, telling her that either Joe or her grandfather or both were already up and about. She got out of bed and slipped her arms into her bathrobe, tying the belt above what used to be her waistline. Then, her feet in her slippers, she made a quick stop in the bathroom before making her way to the kitchen.

Joe stood near the coffeemaker, mug in hand, waiting for the machine to make its last gasp.

"Good morning," she said.

He glanced over his shoulder and grinned. "Morning." As he spoke, he reached over to the stove and turned on the burner beneath the teakettle.

It made her throat tighten, watching him, thinking how nice it was to have someone who knew her so well that he anticipated what she wanted, almost before she knew it herself.

If only...

Joe poured himself a cup of coffee, then turned to face her. "By any chance have you seen my brush? It isn't on the bathroom counter where I thought I left it, and it isn't in the drawer, either."

"Sorry. I haven't seen it."

"Mind if I use yours until I have a chance to buy another?"

"No. I don't mind. Help yourself."

"Can't figure it out." He seemed to be speaking more to himself than to her. "I never used to lose things the way I have since I got here."

Alicia turned away, making herself busy with a

mug and teabag, not wanting Joe to see that she'd lost something since he came here, too.

Her heart.

Joe had been a teenager the last time he'd driven this highway through the mountains to Idaho City. It had been winter then, too, and he and a bunch of his friends, as many as they could pack into one vehicle, had spent the day tubing at the gulch, followed by a swim at the hot springs. If memory served, his driving was more conservative on this trip than on the last.

"You're grinning," Alicia said. "What's funny?"

He released a low chuckle. "I was thinking what a wonder it is that anybody grows older than sixteen."

The words were scarcely out of his mouth when a souped-up, low-slung automobile came barreling up the road behind him. The driver—male, under twenty and stupid—laid on the horn, then passed Joe's SUV seconds before the road curved to the right. Alicia gasped as the car fishtailed before disappearing from view.

"See what I mean?"

She didn't reply, but he sensed her tension. He let up on the gas pedal, hoping to reassure her.

"Were you a reckless teenager?" she asked after a lengthy period of silence.

"Reckless enough."

"I don't remember that about you. You seemed

grown-up, so responsible and mature. You were always doing nice things for Belinda."

"Not always." He tried to remember the last time he'd talked to his sister. "I was as rotten to her as my mom let me get away with."

"I envied her. She never got lonely the way I did. She always had her big brother to talk to."

He cast a quick glance in her direction. "Were you lonely a lot?"

"Oh, I don't suppose you could call it a lot. But sometimes…"

He wished he remembered the child she'd been better than he did; the memories were fuzzy at best. She'd been a girl of ten, skinny, freckled, hair worn in twin braids down her back. His little sister's friend.

At seventeen, the only girls he'd noticed were the ones with short skirts or tight jeans, preferably with hormones racing as fast as his own.

"You're grinning again."

This time his laugh was boisterous.

"What?"

"I think I'll take the Fifth. I want you speaking to me when we get to Idaho City."

"Hmm."

Her murmur of suspicion only made his grin broaden.

"Humphrey Harris," she said in a stage whisper, "no matter how many little brothers or sisters you have, you must promise not to be as rotten to them as Joe was to Belinda."

He felt a peculiar flash of disappointment when she used the name Harris with Humphrey. Better not to analyze why.

"Oh, look!" Alicia's hand lightly touched his right arm. "Joe, slow down. Look up there. On your left."

He followed her commands and saw a small herd of elk on the hillside. The bull raised its head to stare at the highway.

Joe whistled beneath his breath. "Look at the rack on that fellow." He pulled to the side of the road and stopped.

"Isn't he magnificent?"

"Sure is. Think of the hunting seasons he's made it through unscathed. He's gotta be old to have that many points."

"Are you a hunter?" She didn't sound accusatory, only curious.

He shrugged. "Some. Never seem to have enough time. But I enjoy a good elk steak when I can get it."

"Well, I'm glad no hunter's shot that one."

"Me, too." He looked at Alicia. "Because then I couldn't have shared him with you."

They reached Idaho City before eleven. Not unexpectedly, the streets in this former gold rush town in the central Idaho mountains were quiet. Tomorrow, a Saturday, would be different. Folks from the valley would come up for trees or sledding, cross-country skiing, snowmobiling or a relaxing swim at the hot springs. But today it was the locals whose four-wheel-drive vehicles were parked in front of the various business establishments, few as they were.

"Where to now?" Alicia asked.

She leaned closer to the window and looked at the high walls of dirty snow the plows had left on either side of the road. It was difficult to see most of the buildings because of it.

"The paper said I could get directions at the Gold Bar Saloon."

"Not the ranger station?"

"You know how it is in these small towns. Nobody does things the way you expect." Joe turned off the main drag and slowed to a mere crawl. "There it is."

The Gold Bar Saloon was not much more than a large, faded sign and a false storefront. Judging by its exterior, it had to be one of the surviving buildings from the late 1800s.

Joe parked his vehicle in front of the saloon. "Need to use the restroom?"

"Yes. I'd better." She pressed a hand into the small of her back. "Besides, I need to stretch a bit."

"Sit tight. I'll come around for you."

Alicia smiled to herself. She had to admit this sort of service was one of the few perks of being pregnant. Even men who would never otherwise *think* of opening a door for a woman had been opening doors for her for the past couple of months. They also pulled out chairs and allowed her to move ahead in a line.

She was going to miss the many small courtesies once they stopped.

Joe opened the passenger-side door. "Here we go."

She took hold of his hand, and he helped her to the ground. Immediately he took hold of her arm with a firm grasp. She'd grown to like that, too, Joe walking close, protecting her.

Once inside the dilapidated building, he paused to let their eyes adjust to the dim light. Then he said, "There's the restroom. You go ahead. I'll get directions and meet you back here."

She didn't argue with him, suddenly in a hurry, in the way of all expectant mothers. But hurrying didn't turn out to be an easy thing. Not dressed as she was in several layers of clothes. Why on earth had she purchased a pair of bibbed maternity snow pants?

As she reached beneath her oversize sweater and bulky down coat to release the straps from their clasps, she caught sight of herself in the mirror. No one *that* big should have to go through such crazy gyrations, she thought. And then she chuckled. At this rate she would still be in the restroom an hour from now.

What was keeping her? Joe wondered. If she didn't speed things up, they were going to miss their scheduled departure to the lodge. He glanced at his watch again, then back at the restroom door.

"Come on, Alicia. Get a move on."

As if on cue, the door opened, and out she came, smiling as if someone had told her a joke.

"Ready?"

She arched an eyebrow at his impatient tone. Her smile faded. "Why? Are the trees going somewhere?"

"No." But he wanted to keep his secret a little longer. "Guess I'm afraid Christmas will get here before we're ready." He took hold of her arm. "Can't let that happen."

"Do we have time for me to get something to drink? I was hoping—"

"I think there's a store up the road a ways. We'll stop there."

"But I'm thirsty. Can't I—"

He pretended not to hear. He steered her out the saloon doorway, to his vehicle and into the passenger seat. When he settled behind the wheel, he could feel her staring at him in confusion. He didn't return the look. He was afraid he would spoil the surprise if he did.

He pulled onto the street. When he reached the highway, he turned north again, heading higher into the mountains. They drove in silence, and he assumed she was mad at him for refusing to get her a beverage. He couldn't blame her, but hoped she would forgive him once they reached their destination.

The road curved, and suddenly there was a huge

sign. Christmas Sleigh Rides, it proclaimed. A red arrow guided him to a parking lot cut out of the forest.

"Joe?"

He dared to glance her way as the SUV rolled to a stop.

"Merry Christmas, Alicia."

He would have been hard-pressed to describe what the look in her eyes made him feel.

"Oh, Joe."

"Surprised?"

"Yes." There were tears in her eyes and the brightest of smiles on her mouth.

Then he knew what he felt like…like somebody's hero. Like *Alicia's* hero.

"I thought we were getting a tree?" she said softly.

"We are." He shut off the engine, unfastened his seat belt, and opened his door. "A tree and a whole lot more. Come on. You'll see."

It was one of the best days of her life.

Three couples and the driver rode in a bright red sleigh that was pulled by a pair of draft horses with thick winter coats and flowing manes and tails. The steady but muffled beat of their hooves matched the rhythm of jingling bells on the rigging. Otherwise, the snow-covered mountains were silent.

Beneath a layer of plaid woolen blankets, Alicia snuggled against Joe's side, enjoying the passing countryside almost as much as the feel of his arm around her shoulders.

She couldn't get over that he'd done this for her. That he'd plotted and planned, keeping it a secret. She had to remind herself not to make Joe's surprise into more than he'd intended it to be.

"Warm enough?" he asked her.

"Yes." But she snuggled closer, anyway.

"Look over there, folks."

Alicia reluctantly moved her head from Joe's shoulder, following the driver's outstretched arm with her gaze. She was just in time to see a fox darting across a clearing, a reddish-brown blur against the white landscape.

"He's not the only one looking for something to eat," the driver said, pointing again, this time upward.

"What is it?" the woman behind Alicia asked.

"Prairie falcon."

The bird soared effortlessly, as if it were suspended from heaven itself.

"He's takin' it easy right now," the driver continued. "But falcons have been known to dive at over two hundred miles an hour. Pesticides and spreadin' cities have about killed 'em off, but they're makin' a comeback. If you've never been, you ought to visit the Birds of Prey Reserve down on the Snake River."

In a low voice Joe said, "Makes a person thankful to be alive, seeing the beauty of God's creation."

"Yes." She glanced at him. "Thank you, Joe."

He smiled, then he kissed her forehead. "I'm having a good time, too."

The driver interrupted again. "We'll be to the lodge soon. It's around the next bend."

Alicia was sorry to hear it. She didn't want this ride to end.

As if he'd read her thoughts, Joe tightened his arm and said, "The day's not over yet."

Chapter Fifteen

The focal point of the lodge's cavernous main room was a stone fireplace. A blazing fire on the grate greeted the cold but cheerful group when they entered the lodge.

Like the others with her, Alicia looked around, delighted by everything she saw.

The hardwood floor was scuffed and scratched, worn from years of use. Rustic log beams ran the length of the ceiling. Near the center of the room, three round tables had been set with red tablecloths, white tapers in crystal candleholders, and plates with a pattern of holly and mistletoe painted around the edges. A pair of Christmas trees, draped with garlands of red, green and silver, added to the festive decor. Familiar carols played over loudspeakers decorated with tinsel and candy canes, and delicious odors wafted from the adjoining kitchen area.

Joe leaned close to Alicia. "Notice how they've

placed those Christmas trees. You can't see the other tables. They're giving each couple their privacy."

His warm breath on her neck caused goose pimples to rise on her arm.

"Hope you like barbecue," he added.

"I do."

"It seemed more of a summertime offering to me, but I guess it goes with the surroundings."

She looked at him. "It's perfect. Everything's perfect."

His grin made it even more so.

A large man—easily six foot four, with a girth that matched his height—came through a pair of swinging doors from the kitchen, a Santa hat perched on his head.

"Welcome folks. Come on in. Come on in." He motioned with his hands. "That's right. Take yourselves over by the fire and get warm. I'm Harold, owner of the Nugget Lodge. This here's my wife, Marisa."

A woman about half her husband's size stepped from behind him, flashing a bright smile at one and all. She wore a Santa hat, too.

"You just give your coats to Marisa," Harold continued, "and then make yourselves at home. We'll have your dinners out in no time. Sure hope you're hungry." With that he turned and strode into the kitchen.

Marisa came forward with an outstretched arm. "Let me take your coats. Did you stay warm enough in the sleigh? Did you see any deer? How about elk? See any of them?" She kept talking without giving anyone a chance to answer her questions.

Alicia exchanged an amused glance with Joe as she handed her coat to the woman.

"Well, look at you!" Marisa exclaimed. "About ready to pop, ain't you? When's that baby due?" Finally, an expectant pause.

"Next month," Alicia replied.

Marisa looked at Joe. "You're one lucky man. You take good care of this pretty little mama now." She winked at him, then moved off toward the other couples.

Over the stereo speakers, a new song began to play. It was one of her favorite Christmas carols: "Mary, Did You Know?" As the melody filled the air, she couldn't help imagining Mary and Joseph on a wintry night in Bethlehem many centuries before—tired, hungry, in need of shelter for the night, Mary large with child. Had Mary often wondered about what the future would bring for her precious son, the way Alicia often wondered about her child's future?

She smiled, certain that in many ways, Mary was just like her—a mother who wanted only the very best for the baby she carried in her womb.

Was it possible Alicia had grown prettier over the weeks since Joe first met with her in that coffee shop?

Firelight flickered across her features and streaked

her hair with gold. There was a pretty peach-pink flush in her cheeks and a soft upward curve in the corners of her mouth. Her eyes had turned from aquamarine to midnight-blue in the dimly lit room.

He might have kissed her if the proprietor hadn't poked his head out of the kitchen to announce they should all be seated.

Maybe it was just as well.

The barbecued beef, garlic mashed potatoes, salads and breads, and other side dishes were all delicious. Even better than the article in the paper had described. But it was Joe's charming companion, his wife—however temporary that might be—who made the meal seem like the best he'd ever eaten.

Their conversation centered on childhood Christmases, on memories of other trips to the mountains to ski or sled or visit the hot springs that were in abundance in this area. Alicia told Joe about the time she broke her thumb while sledding on a hillside above Lucky Peak Reservoir. He told her about the time he flew over the moguls at Bogus Basin and crashed—*spectacularly* crashed, he was quick to point out—right in front of the beginners' class by the rope tow. She told him about the Christmas she got a puppy named Rags, a gift from her grandfather. He told her about the year he gave his sister a black eye during a childhood squabble and had to spend the entire Christmas break in his room.

Over dessert—spice cake with cream cheese frosting—she expressed the loneliness of recent holidays. Somewhat surprised by his own admission, he said the same was true for him. Only he'd been too busy to recognize it at the time.

"We won't be lonely this year," she said in a near whisper.

"No. Not this year."

But what about next year?

Joe might have voiced his question aloud if Harold hadn't returned and announced that the sleigh was waiting to take them to chop down their trees.

"Your coats and things are next to the door." He pointed. "When you're done, Gus will bring you back here for hot chocolate or coffee before you head down to the parking lot." Harold waved a farewell, then retreated to the kitchen once again.

"Gus," Alicia said as she looked at Joe. "I wondered what our driver's name was." She smiled, a twinkle in her eyes. "He even looks like a Gus, doesn't he?"

Joe couldn't say he'd given any thought to what a "Gus" was supposed to look like, but he nodded anyway.

"I'd better use the restroom before we go." She rose from her chair. "Don't let the sleigh leave without me."

"I won't."

She walked away, and Joe couldn't help grinning as he watched her, a little waddle in each step. Adorable.

* * *

It took about twenty minutes to reach the tree farm.

Gus brought the sleigh to a halt, then twisted on the driver's seat and said, "Spruce trees are over that way." He pointed. "And the ponderosa pines are over that way." He moved his arm in another direction. "Signs are clearly marked. Trees range from four to eight feet. If you need help, all you need do is ask."

Joe waited until the other couples had disembarked, then he asked Alicia, "Do you want to stay in the sleigh?"

"Not on your life. I want the full experience."

"Okay, but you hang on to me. I don't want you falling."

She was happy to oblige. Holding on to Joe was her favoritemost thing to do...except for kissing him.

"Which type of Christmas tree do you prefer?" he asked as he helped her to the ground.

"Spruce."

"Okay." He selected an ax from the rear of the sleigh. Then, holding it in his right hand, he offered her his left arm. "Let's go."

The trails were well packed, and walking was easier than Alicia had expected it to be. Their boots only made slight impressions in the snow. Still, Joe's pace was slow in deference to her condition.

No wonder I love him.

His head was bare, the tops of his ears were red with the cold, and his thick black hair was wind-blown from the sleigh ride. She could see a faint blue-black shadow beneath the skin on his jaw. In another five hours his cheek would be prickly with a beard's stubble.

Joe stopped walking. "How about that one?" He indicated a tree with his outstretched arm.

She looked, although she'd forgotten they were there for a tree until he reminded her.

"What do you think? Put it in the alcove next to the piano? It'll pretty much fill up the window space there."

"I love it. It's perfect."

No point in telling him she wanted whatever he wanted. If he'd picked a scraggly pine with needles falling off, she would have said it was perfect.

He grinned. "Okay. You stand right here, Ms. Harris, and watch a man do his work." With an exaggerated John Wayne swagger, he walked away from her, the ax handle now resting on his shoulder.

She laughed aloud. "My hero."

"You mock me?" He glanced back at her.

"Never!"

"Good."

As she watched Joe walk around the tree, she thought of something her grandfather had said to her a long time ago. "When God formed you in your mother's womb, Alicia, He already knew the man designed to be your life mate. Wait and watch, dear one. God's plans are always better than the ones we make for ourselves."

Was it possible that Joe was that life mate? She

wanted him to be, with her whole heart. But she'd rushed into things before, never listening to God to see if what she was doing was what He wanted for her. She wanted to change. She wanted to stop and listen.

Your will and not mine, Father. Change me from the inside out.

"Okay," Joe called to her. "Here goes."

He took his first swing. The sound of metal striking wood rang in the forest. He swung again, and wood chips flew through the air. He paused, removed his gloves and shucked off his bulky down coat, then wielded the ax again.

The rhythm of Joe's movements resonated in Alicia's chest. Back swing. Forward swing. *Crack!* Back swing. Forward swing. *Crack!*

She cupped her hands around her mouth and shouted, "You could do this professionally."

He paused, looked her way, grinned. "Maybe I'll give up practicing law and buy a tree farm like this one. What would you think of that? A lodge in the mountains where the snowdrifts pile six or ten feet deep in the winter months and elk come to forage in the front yard?"

Her heart fluttered. Was he including her in that fantasy? All she could do was smile and nod.

Joe was enjoying this more than he'd imagined he would. When the tree toppled, he stared at the fruit of his labor with satisfaction. But before he could see if Alicia was suitably impressed, something cold and wet hit the side of his head.

"What the—?"

Her laughter rang all around him.

He touched his head. Snow? A snowball! She'd thrown a snowball at him.

He turned. She watched him with wide eyes, trying to look innocent.

It didn't work.

"Not a wise thing to do, my dear." He bent down to grab a handful of the white stuff.

"You wouldn't throw a snowball at a pregnant woman, would you?"

He revealed what he hoped was a wicked grin. "You're about to find out."

She turned and started away from him as fast as she could. He might have thought she was afraid, only he heard her laughter again. He took off in pursuit, part of him enjoying the chase, part of him worried about her slipping and falling.

She couldn't hope to outdistance him, and he caught up with her in short order. His hand on her arm stayed her flight. An instant later, he had her wrapped in a tight embrace.

"Foolish woman. I may not pay you back now, but it'll snow again next year. You won't be pregnant then." Too late, he realized what his words implied.

Silence encompassed them. Alicia's eyes swirled with emotions Joe would just as soon not recognize.

He could almost hear her heart beating, almost grasp the breathless anticipation of the moment.

"You confuse me," he whispered, his mouth drawing closer to hers.

"I'm sorry, Joe. That's not my intent."

Even more softly, he said, "I know. That only makes it worse."

He kissed her, long and slow and sweet. Their mingled breaths formed a misty cloud above their heads.

Time stood still.

Joe was treading on dangerous ground. He shouldn't be holding her, kissing her, enjoying her, caring about her. He was all wrong for her. He was all wrong for marriage. There was no future for them, and it would be unfair to let either of them think otherwise.

He drew back, no more than an inch. He planned to tell her again all the reasons why they shouldn't do this. But when he opened his eyes, he found her watching him, and the look she gave him stole the words straight out of his head.

He couldn't think. All he could do was kiss her again.

Alicia allowed hope to return. Her heart soared with it. Her mind sang with it. It pulsed through her veins like lifeblood itself.

When Joe pulled away a second time, his expression was both grim and puzzled. He searched her face with his gaze; she tried to hide what she felt for him by looking away.

"We'd better get back to the sleigh," he said. "The others will be waiting for us."

"Yes."

"I'll get the tree."

"Okay."

"Can you carry the ax?"

"I'm not a weakling."

"I just don't want to take chances."

She glanced at him again. "I know." She felt dangerously close to tears.

He turned on his heel and strode across the snow to where he'd dropped the ax. He picked it up and brought it to her, passing it into her waiting hands without a word. Then he returned to the felled tree. He put on his coat and gloves, keeping his back toward Alicia the entire time. Finally he grasped the tree trunk with both hands and began dragging it in her direction.

"Watch your step," he said as he drew near. "I'll be right behind you."

Why did love have to be so hard? she wondered as she turned toward the sleigh. Why couldn't Joe love her as she loved him?

The memory of his kisses flowed over her, causing her knees to weaken. She stumbled.

"Alicia?"

She raised one hand but didn't look back. "I'm fine." She kept walking.

But she wasn't fine, and she wondered if she would ever be fine again.

Chapter Sixteen

It was after five o'clock by the time Joe pulled his vehicle into the driveway.

After he'd turned the key and the engine fell silent, Alicia said, "Would you mind if we wait to decorate the tree until tomorrow? I'm exhausted."

"No, I don't mind. If that's what you want."

She opened the passenger door. "It is." She stepped down to the sidewalk, shoveled clear of snow. Then she looked back at him. "Thanks for the wonderful day, Joe. I'll remember it always."

"Sure thing."

He frowned as he watched her walk toward the back porch, a hand in the small of her back. Maybe he shouldn't have taken her up there. Maybe she'd done too much.

But deep down, he knew that wasn't what bothered her.

Regret washed over him. Had their outing today

been motivated by his good intentions or by selfishness? He no longer knew. What he did know was that he'd managed to hurt her again. Was this in some way the result of the lies they'd told her grandfather?

"Lord, she acted out of love for him. Was it so wrong?"

Heavyhearted, he got out of the SUV. A short while later, he leaned the pine tree against the side of the house near the back door, then went inside.

Grandpa Roger sat at the table, a steaming bowl of stew in front of him, along with a small loaf of home-baked bread.

Joe acknowledged him with a nod, then glanced toward the doorway to the living room.

"She went to bed," her grandfather said.

"Maybe this wasn't such a good idea, going up there."

"She told me she had a wonderful time."

Joe looked toward the older man but didn't reply.

"There's more stew on the stove." Grandpa Roger motioned toward it. "A friend of mine made it and the bread. You're welcome to help yourself. It's good."

"I should check on Alicia first. I'll be back."

Moments later he looked into the bedroom and found her already in bed, the blankets pulled almost over her head. Her maternity wear—bibbed ski pants and oversize slipover sweater—had been dropped on a chair, and her boots and socks had been set beneath it.

He stepped back and closed the door, then returned to the kitchen. A place had been set for him at the table, and he joined Alicia's grandfather there.

"So tell me about your day. Alicia didn't go into details."

It was easier to talk about the day's activities than to think about his feelings for Alicia, so Joe was willing to oblige. He talked about the wildlife they'd seen, about the sleigh ride, about the lodge and its proprietor and his wife, about the tree farm, even about the snowball Alicia had thrown at him.

And when he'd run out of things to say, he asked, "What did you do all day, sir?"

"Took it easy." Grandpa Roger scooted his chair back from the table, then reached into the pocket of his sweater vest. "I have something for you." He withdrew a blue velvet box from his pocket and set it on the table. "Open it."

Joe picked it up. He cast a questioning glance at the old man.

"Go on. Open it."

He obeyed, lifting the lid to reveal an antique pocket watch. The gold hunting case bore the image of an elk, intricately etched into the surface. Time had smoothed the craftsman's work but not destroyed it.

"It was my grandfather's. Then it was my father's. Then it was mine. Then it was my son's."

Joe removed it from the box and opened the case.

"Cost more than forty dollars. That was a lot of money in its day. Twenty ruby jewels in gold settings,

Breguet hairspring double-sunk dial, fourteen-karat-gold-filled case. It came with a twenty-year guarantee. Still runs, too, when the stem is wound."

"It's great, sir." Joe looked from the watch in his hand to Grandpa Roger.

"It's for you to give to your son."

A lump formed in Joe's throat, and he had to look away.

"It's tradition for it to go to the firstborn male in each generation. I was going to give it to Alicia to keep until she has a son the right age, but…well, now that you're part of the family, I'd like you to hang on to it."

"And if this baby isn't a boy?"

Grandpa Roger chuckled. "There comes a time when even good traditions should be broken. Probably should have gone to Alicia when she turned eighteen. You can give it to your daughter, if that's what you choose. Just keep it in the family. That's all I ask. A reminder of those who've gone before."

Joe was an impostor. He had no right to be holding this family heirloom.

"It's not the most important legacy to pass on, of course."

Joe lifted an eyebrow in question.

"Faith, my boy. Teach your children to choose the right path, and when they are older, they will remain upon it. Nothing you impart to them will be more important than their faith and trust in Jesus Christ."

Joe nodded. It was a legacy his parents hadn't

been able to give him. They'd had no faith of their own to share. But if he were to become a father—

He broke off the thought. Better not to go there in his imagination.

Roger Harris leaned forward and touched the back of Joe's hand. "Don't tell Alicia I gave you the watch. She might think it means my health is failing. You've seen how she frets over me."

"Yes, sir."

"I thought we'd settled this 'sir' business."

"Tough habit to break." Joe shrugged, offering a weak smile. "I called my dad 'sir.' He expected it."

"Well, see if you can't manage to break the habit before I head back to Arizona." Grandpa Roger rose with a soft groan. "Wouldn't think I'd be so tired after doing nothing all day, but I am. I'm turning in." He reached for his bowl and empty milk glass.

"Just leave the dishes. I'll take care of them."

"Thanks, my boy."

Long after Grandpa Roger left the kitchen, Joe sat staring at the watch and wondering how he would feel if he really were the baby's father.

Although Alicia was forced by her condition to get up frequently in the night, it wasn't until she awakened early the next morning that she realized Joe hadn't slept on the bedroom sofa.

She tried not to feel alarmed. After all, there was no rule that said he *had* to share her bedroom. But it worried her, anyway.

As soon as she finished in the bathroom, she went looking for him. She found him in the basement, asleep in his makeshift office, his head cradled on his arms atop his desk.

"Joe?" She touched his shoulder.

He awakened slowly, blinking his eyes, straightening with a groan, a look of confusion on his face.

"Did you stay down here all night?"

"I guess so." He glanced around the cramped room, as if making certain he knew where he was. "I must've fallen asleep while I was working."

Alicia didn't know whether to be disappointed or relieved.

Joe stretched and yawned while scratching his head. "I got a letter from a law firm in Boise. I discovered it with the rest of the mail after your grandfather went to bed last night." He glanced toward his laptop. When he touched the pad, the black screen vanished, replaced by a calendar program. "They want to meet with me next week. I was working on my portfolio and must've decided to rest my eyes. That's the last thing I remember."

"Are you pleased about it?"

"They're one of the top firms in Idaho. I'd be lucky to get on with them."

Alicia sat on the chair on the opposite side of the desk, pulling her robe closed over her stomach. "They'd be the lucky ones."

"You're prejudiced."

I'm supposed to be. I'm your wife.

More awake now, he gave her a tender smile. "You always look cute in the mornings. You know that?"

"Don't be silly," she replied, flustered by the unexpected compliment. She pushed her tousled hair away from her face with one hand. "I'm a sight."

"I think it's those bunny slippers." He rose and peered over the desk at her feet. "Yup, it's those slippers."

Her heart performed crazy palpitations in response to his teasing words.

"If you'll tell me where you keep your Christmas decorations, we can decorate the tree after I have my coffee." He yawned and stretched again. "Only a week left until Christmas. No time to waste."

One week until Christmas. Two weeks until her grandfather returned to Arizona. And then Joe would leave, too.

How she wished she could make time stand still.

"Alicia? The decorations?"

She stood as quickly as she was able. "In the storage closet at the foot of the stairs. The boxes are clearly marked." She turned toward the door. "I'll start the coffee brewing."

"This is one of my personal favorites," Grandpa Roger said, holding out an ornament for Joe to see. "Alicia made this at Sunday school when she was about seven or eight."

Joe took the shellacked, walnut half-shell ornament. Inside was a miniature doll covered by a piece of burlap. It looked like a baby in a cradle. On the bottom, in tiny lettering—obviously not that of a child—had been painted "John 3:16." Gold thread was attached at both ends so it could be hung on a tree.

"It's meant to be baby Jesus in the manger," Grandpa Roger finished.

Joe stared into the box on the table. "Looks like making decorations was an annual pastime."

"It was." Alicia came to stand beside him. "My mom loved to do crafts."

"So that's where you got it."

She raised an eyebrow in question.

Joe motioned with an arm. "Your entire house is filled with those little touches." He lowered his voice. "The things that make a place feel like a home."

An attractive flush rose in her cheeks.

His throat felt tight as he added, "I never paid much attention to that kind of stuff before I came here."

She smiled, a look as warm and comforting as the home she'd made for herself.

He thought about kissing her.

Then he thought better of it.

As if sensing his decision, she returned to the box Joe had placed on the sofa. "Remember bubble lights?" she asked, lifting a string of them. "I think these are older than I am."

"They most certainly are," her grandfather said. "Teresa bought those when your father was a boy.

My goodness. How very long ago that was. Do they still work?"

Alicia plugged them into the outlet, and they lit up. "They do." She looked and sounded as excited as a child. "Watch and see how long it takes for them to start bubbling."

She would be the sort of mother who made Christmas special for her children, Joe thought, looking at her rather than the lights. She would bake cookies and build snowmen. She would hide wrapped packages all over the house. She would tell her children bedtime stories, and she would probably be as sleepless as the little ones on Christmas Eve.

Joe's mother hadn't made cookies or snowmen, hadn't hidden packages, hadn't told bedtime stories. He supposed she had done the best she could, but her loneliness had affected the way she approached the holidays. He couldn't remember a Christmas his dad hadn't gone to his office for at least part of the day. Of course, there'd been plenty of toys and other presents. That's how his mother had tried to make up for everything else that was lacking.

But Alicia's baby would have different memories. *Lucky kid.*

Joe looked across the room and watched as Alicia began stringing lights on the tree. She moved awkwardly, her extended belly often in the way. It made Joe smile, thinking again how cute she looked.

A very lucky kid.

* * *

Decorating the Christmas tree had been an event in her parents' home, and Alicia had tried to continue the tradition, even in the years when she'd been alone for the holidays. But this Christmas she was with Grandpa and Joe. That made it even more special.

They paused often in their decorating to reminisce. Almost every ornament had a memory tied to it. Grandpa Roger was a superb storyteller, and he was in his element today, regaling them with one tale after another. He seemed to take particular pleasure in telling Joe about Alicia's childhood escapades.

She lost track of the number of times Joe's gaze met with hers. Each time it happened, her pulse skittered and raced. It was obvious she'd failed in her effort to think of him as a friend. She might not be allowed to tell him she loved him, but her heart wasn't fooled. Not for a moment.

When they finished, the last ornament in place atop the tree, the three of them stood back, Alicia between the two men, and admired their handiwork.

"I don't believe I've seen a better tree in all my born days," Grandpa Roger said with the voice of authority.

"I think maybe you're right." Joe slipped his arm around Alicia's shoulders.

She could only smile in pure, unadulterated bliss.

"You know what we need now?" Her grandfather looked at her. "Hot, spiced apple cider."

"Oh, Grandpa, how could I forget? I'll have to run to the store."

"No, you won't," he said. "I had Joe pick up everything we need last week."

"You did?"

Joe squeezed her shoulders. "Cider. Cinnamon sticks. Cloves, I think. Was there something else?" He turned toward the kitchen, steering her with him. "Come on. I'll help you."

Happiness flowed through her, warm and inviting. She would treasure the memory of this day for the rest of her life.

Her vision blurred, but she managed to reply in a normal voice, "Great. I'd love your help."

While Alicia retrieved a large pot from the cupboard near the stove, Joe brought a paper grocery bag in from the back porch.

"I've got a gallon of cider. Want the whole thing in there?"

"Please."

As he poured the golden brown liquid into the pot, Joe said, "I meant to tell you. I hired someone to come in next week and finish the nursery wallpapering." He glanced at her. "No comment?"

She smiled. "No comment."

"Good."

Alicia turned on the electric burner beneath the pot, then added several cinnamon sticks to the cider.

"I bet you'll be glad when the waiting is over."

"Waiting?"

"For the baby to be born."

His comment surprised her, but she tried not to show it. "These last weeks have seemed long."

"You've never said if you want a boy or a girl."

"Yes." She smiled. "I want a boy or a girl."

He chuckled. "I walked into that one, didn't I?"

"Uh-huh."

"You must need more for the nursery than what's in there now. When do you plan to finish setting it up?"

It was the sort of conversation Alicia imagined any expectant couple might have while they stood together in the kitchen. His words made her heart flutter with happiness; she yearned for it to be real.

"Soon," she answered, hoping her emotions weren't revealed in her voice. "Everything's in stock except for the cradle I want. The supplier promised he'll be able to deliver it by mid-January. That should be in time. First babies often come late."

"I didn't know that." He spoke softly. "But then, I didn't know much about babies before I was married to you."

Their gazes met and held for a heartbeat.

She thought he might say more.

He remained silent.

"How's that cider coming?" Grandpa Roger called from the other room.

The moment was lost.

Alicia looked toward the stove. "It needs to simmer at least an hour to be good, Grandpa."

"You know—" Joe cleared his throat as he took a step back from the counter "—if it's going to be that long, I think I'll clear up some work on my desk, maybe check my email. Call me when it's ready."

"Okay."

The kitchen felt much too large, much too empty after he left.

Joe didn't accomplish a thing. He spent the next hour staring at a blank computer screen and wondering what was going on with him. He didn't know his own mind anymore, and that was an uncomfortable condition for his personality type. He liked knowing what he wanted and then going after it. But now…

He was relieved when Alicia called down to him that the spiced cider was ready, glad for any interruption to his troubled thoughts.

He rolled the chair back from the desk and started to rise. He wasn't sure what caused him to glance at the top of the two-drawer filing cabinet beside the desk where his day planner should have been—and wasn't.

He frowned. What had he done with it? He checked in the corner behind him, then under the desk, then behind the open door. No sign of it.

"Maybe I put it in the bedroom."

"Joe? Did you hear me? The cider's ready."

"Coming."

He swept the tiny office with his gaze one more

time, as if hoping the day planner would miraculously appear.

It didn't.

When he reached the kitchen, he asked Alicia, "Have you seen my planner anywhere? About this big. Black cowhide."

"Wasn't it next to your desk? I'm sure I saw it there this morning."

Joe's scowl deepened. "That's what I thought." He turned toward the living room. "I'm going to check in the bedroom."

He looked everywhere to no avail. It wasn't long before both Alicia and her grandfather were involved in the search, but they were no more successful than Joe. The day planner had vanished.

"Something's going on." He left the bedroom for the third time and walked down the hall toward the living room.

He found Alicia on her knees, looking behind the Christmas tree, her backside stuck up in the air, her belly touching the floor, the ears of her pink bunny slippers flattened against the hardwood.

The sight made him chuckle.

She straightened, turning toward the sound. Joe expected a tongue-lashing, but instead, he heard a sharp gasp. A look of pain tightened her features.

He hurried across the room. "What's wrong?"

"I moved too fast is all. But I think I pulled a muscle in my back."

"You shouldn't have been down there in the first

place." He took hold of both her arms and drew her to her feet.

A groan slipped from between her tightly pressed lips, although he could tell she'd done her best not to let it happen.

"You'd better lie down."

"The cider—" she began.

"The cider can wait. Come on."

As he turned her toward the bedroom, one arm around her back, the other holding her elbow, he discovered Grandpa Roger observing them from the kitchen doorway.

"I'm okay, Grandpa."

He ignored her and asked Joe, "Should we call the doctor?"

"I don't know."

"Would you two listen to me? I'm okay. I just need a few minutes to rest."

"Stubborn, like your grandmother," Grandpa Roger retorted.

"More like my grandpa," she whispered so only Joe could hear.

He suppressed a smile and kept her moving toward the bedroom.

"This is *so* silly, Joe. I can see myself to bed."

"I don't mind. Besides, it's my fault you're in pain. If I hadn't misplaced my planner, you wouldn't have been on the floor like that."

They reached the side of the bed. Joe turned down the blankets and sheet, then plumped the pillows.

"Lie down and stay there until you feel better."

She tilted her head to one side and narrowed her eyes as she looked up at him. "You're getting mighty bossy, Mr. Palermo."

"You haven't begun to see how bossy I can be. You've been having twinges and pains for a couple of weeks now. You keep saying it's normal, but I'm not so sure. Come Monday, I think you'd better see your doctor."

She must have seen he meant business for she sighed and nodded. "All right. Next week is my checkup, anyway. Now go make sure Grandpa doesn't worry himself sick over this. It's nothing."

Chapter Seventeen

The ache in Alicia's lower back came and went all the rest of the day. Sometimes it didn't feel like much. Other times it hurt like the dickens. But at least she convinced Joe and Grandpa Roger that she was feeling herself again.

Feeling herself.

When was the last time *that* had been an accurate description? She didn't know what "herself" should feel like.

Just what was normal?

It began to snow again on Sunday afternoon. Joe shoveled the walks three different times and spread ice melt as an extra safeguard. Alicia decided the least she could do was find his missing planner. However, there would be no more crawling on the floor.

Standing at the bottom of the stairs, she stared toward Joe's office. He wasn't a careless sort. On the contrary, he was well-organized. He wouldn't misplace his day planner. Since he'd come to live in her house, she'd seen him make numerous entries into that black book. She knew how important it was to him.

So what happened to it? She couldn't imagine a thief coming into her home and stealing a planner while leaving a laptop and other valuables. No, there was no thief to blame. So who?

"Think," she said to herself.

Rosie rubbed against Alicia's shin, then serpentined between and around her ankles in two perfect figure eights.

"Sorry, girl. I'm too tired to bend over and pick you up."

Rosie meowed her complaint, then dashed up the stairs in a huff. Rags galloped out of the shadows at the opposite end of the basement. She whisked past Alicia in a blur of white and gray, giving chase to the cat.

"Rags! Stop right now."

All Alicia needed was for those two to knock something over.

"Sit!"

The dog halted at the top of the stairs. She turned and plopped down on her back haunches, looking totally unrepentant.

"Rags," Alicia began to scold.

And then she stopped.

Surely not.

She flipped one of the switches on the nearby wall. Bare bulbs cast an unforgiving light throughout the large main room of the basement. The floor was concrete, the walls plasterboarded but never finished out. Alicia rarely came down here. Until Joe set up his office in the room near the furnace, she'd had little reason to.

But Rags and Rosie had full run of the house, including the basement.

Alicia walked to the opposite end of the room. On an old, tattered blanket that the dog was obviously using for a bed, she saw not only the remains of a day planner, but also Joe's missing hairbrush, pen and glove, plus some items he hadn't yet discovered were missing.

"Oh, Rags. What have you done?"

With care, she bent down to pick up the binder. The expensive leather had been chewed like a rawhide toy. Pages had been ripped from the rings and were scattered everywhere. Some were so mauled there was no hope of knowing what had been written on them.

She heard the back door slam. Boots stomped on the floor overhead. Joe had finished shoveling the walks.

She closed her eyes. He'd never liked her animals. He barely tolerated them. Maybe it would be better if she didn't tell him what she'd found.

But that wasn't a real option.

"No time like the present," she said aloud as she started up the stairs.

Joe placed the mug of spiced cider in the microwave, closed the door and hit Start. The machine hummed for thirty seconds before he heard the familiar *ding*. But before he could retrieve his beverage, he heard the telltale squeak of the top step on the basement stairs. He looked over his shoulder.

Alicia's gaze met his, then dropped away.

Now what? Living with her, it was always something.

"I found your planner."

"Where?"

She let out a breath. "Rags had it."

"Rags?"

She nodded before holding out his black binder. "I'm so sorry, Joe." She straightened her arm, urging him to take the destroyed planner.

He opened the cover. The year's planning calendars were missing, as were several other sections.

"I guess she likes you."

"Likes me?"

"Your other things are down there, too."

"What other things?" The words were barely out of his mouth before he remembered—his pen, his glove, his brush. "Never mind."

"I *am* sorry. Rags didn't mean to do anything

wrong. I—" She offered an anemic smile. "I'm serious. I think she has a crush on you."

Stupid pets! His thought was automatic, but after a moment he recognized it was out of habit, not because he was angry or irritated. In fact, what he wanted to do was grin—so he did.

"Why don't you show me this evidence of your mutt's affection?"

She didn't say so, but he knew his lack of anger surprised her. Almost as much as it surprised him. Then he wondered what that said about him as a person. Nothing good.

"Is it in the basement?" He motioned toward the stairs. "Might as well show me."

"You're not angry?"

"Surprised, huh?"

"Yes." Her reply was honest, but it came with another small smile.

"No more so than me."

Their gazes held a short while longer. Joe wondered what she was thinking behind those pretty eyes of hers. He might have asked in a few more heartbeats, but she turned away and he lost his chance.

Rags seemed to know she'd stepped over the line of acceptable behavior. For the remainder of the day she shadowed Joe, even going so far as to lay her head on his thigh while he sat at his desk, piecing together those planner pages that could be salvaged.

"I should wring your neck, you mangy no-good hound."

Rags whimpered.

"That's not going to get you any sympathy."

How was it a dog could look repentant despite all that hair covering its eyes?

"What's happened to my life, Rags? Nothing's going the way it was supposed to. Nothing."

As soon as the ten o'clock news concluded that evening, Alicia's grandfather rose from his chair and announced he was off to bed.

"Sleep well, Grandpa."

"The same to you both. See you in the morning." He disappeared into the hallway.

Alicia drew a deep breath and released it slowly. "It feels much later than 10:30, doesn't it?" She glanced at Joe, seated beside her on the sofa.

"I ought to sleep good tonight. All that snow shoveling I did today."

"You've worked hard ever since you got here."

He shrugged.

A sharp, quick pain stabbed her in the small of her back, and she gasped.

"Your back again?" Joe asked.

She nodded.

"I'm taking you to the doctor's tomorrow." He turned off the television, plunging the room into semidarkness, the only illumination coming from the red, green and white lights on the tree. "For now, would a back rub help?"

"Maybe." She looked at him but couldn't see his

eyes in the darkness of the room. "But would you mind just holding me instead?"

He was silent a long while before saying, "No, I don't mind." His arm went about her shoulders and drew her close, her head resting on his chest.

Ecstasy and heartache warred inside her, the joy of the present and the dread of the future mingling together, creating emotional havoc. She swallowed the lump in her throat, determined not to cry, determined not to spoil the moment. Joe's heart beat a steady rhythm beneath her ear, a comforting sound in the silence of the room.

Oh, how she wished they could remain like this forever. If only...

Alicia was surprised when she awakened to a bedroom flooded with daylight. She didn't remember coming to bed last night. How late had she and Joe stayed up? Something told her he'd held her for hours.

She smiled to herself, a bittersweet smile that mirrored the feeling in her heart. How wonderful to be held as if she were loved. How sad not to be loved even while held.

But she refused to dwell on such thoughts. Not today. Like Scarlett O'Hara, she would think about it tomorrow. Or in her case, after her grandfather returned to Arizona and Joe moved out of the house for good.

Slowly—for it seemed she could do nothing in

haste these days—she sat up, lowering her legs over the side of the bed. It was only as she started to rise to her feet that she realized the pain in her back was gone. Not so much as a tiny ache or twinge.

She could hardly wait to tell Joe. But as it turned out, she wasn't able to tell him anything.

"He got a phone call while we were having breakfast," Grandpa Roger told her a short while later. "He said he'll be gone about an hour or two. And he wanted me to remind you to call your doctor."

"It's not necessary. My back isn't bothering me at all this morning."

"I don't think that'll matter much to your husband. He was adamant about you seeing your doctor today."

"I've got an appointment on Wednesday. That's soon enough."

"Young folk." Grandpa Roger shook his head. "I guess you'll have to work that out between the two of you." He set aside the novel he'd been reading and rose from the easy chair. "Right now, let's get you some breakfast."

It was the sort of apartment Joe'd had in mind for himself. Two bedrooms, one to sleep in and one he could use for an office when he worked late at home. Large windows and high ceilings. All the modern kitchen conveniences. A gas fireplace—no muss, no fuss. Reasonably quick access to downtown and the courthouse. A view of the river from the living room; a view of the mountains from the master bedroom. A swimming pool, racquetball court, tennis court, workout room.

One problem, however—this was the only available unit and nothing was scheduled for vacancy in the next few months. If he wanted to live in this complex, he'd have to rent the apartment today. It would be gone by tomorrow.

He stared out the large window at the snow-bordered Boise River, frowning slightly.

It wasn't as if he couldn't afford to rent the place now and leave it empty for a couple of weeks. Besides, he could make arrangements for the movers to deliver his furniture between now and then. That way everything would be ready for him right on schedule.

He turned toward the rental manager. "I'll take it."

"Wonderful," Ms. Barton, an attractive woman in her early thirties, said with a smile. "Come to my office. Since you're a lawyer, I'm sure you know there's always plenty of paperwork to be seen to."

Once in the office he studied every word, every clause, of the lease before he signed it, but the memory of Alicia falling asleep in his arms last night kept intruding, breaking his concentration. He was relieved when he could write the deposit and first month's rent check, hand it to Ms. Barton, and be on his way.

So why didn't he feel better now that he'd found a place to live?

That question played in his head over and over again as he drove toward home.

Home...

Therein lay the answer. The apartment he'd rented wouldn't be home. Home was a drafty farmhouse with an attack cat who hissed at him and a mangy dog who stole things and chewed them to bits. Home had a Christmas tree decorated with homemade ornaments and a string of ancient bubble lights. Home had a kitchen with yellow walls, lace curtains at the windows, a Formica and chrome table and ugly vinyl-covered chairs.

Home had all those things.

It also had Alicia.

Joe pulled his vehicle to the side of the road and cut the engine. Silence filled the interior of the SUV.

Home, he realized, had nothing to do with the building or the things in it. Home from now on would be wherever Alicia was.

He didn't want to live in an apartment with all the modern conveniences. He didn't need a view of the river or the mountains, a swimming pool or a racquetball court.

What he needed and wanted was Alicia.

He shook his head, marveling at the certainty he felt. This must have been what God had in mind for him from the very start. How else could Joe have found himself back in Idaho, willing to trade the peace of his former life for a future filled with the chaos of parenthood, filled with 2:00 a.m. feedings and diaper changes, with Rosie the attack cat and with Rags, the collector and destroyer of his personal possessions?

And with Alicia. Alicia, who had become as important to him as the air he breathed.

He grinned. The wonder of this day wasn't that he'd found the perfect apartment. The real wonder was that Joe had fallen in love with his wife.

Now all he needed was to find the right moment to tell her he wanted their marriage to be more than make-believe, more than a temporary situation. He wanted it to be forever.

Chapter Eighteen

The final few days before Christmas flew by.

Grandpa Roger had a friend take him out for some last-minute shopping. "Secrets are a part of the season" was the explanation he gave Alicia.

Joe went to his job interview and seemed pleased afterward. "I believe they'll ask me to join the firm. Looks like a good fit."

Alicia stayed busy, too, wrapping gifts, baking cookies and beginning to put the nursery in order after the wallpapering was finished. But her small world seemed off-kilter somehow, though she couldn't say precisely how or why. Perhaps it was the way Joe watched her whenever they were together, as if she were a puzzle to be solved.

On Christmas Eve, Grandpa Roger, Alicia and Joe attended the candlelight service at church. It was another special memory for her to treasure in her heart. Perhaps all the more so because she realized how soon both Joe and her grandfather would be leaving, how few memories she still had time to gather.

Upon their return home, Alicia filled large Santa mugs with hot chocolate, and the three of them sat in the living room, watching the bubble lights and sipping their beverages. For a time each was lost in private thoughts.

It was Grandpa Roger who broke the silence. "What about the baby's name? Have you two come to an agreement yet?"

"Not yet," Alicia answered.

"You're running out of time, you know."

"We know."

She hated the lies. They seemed to pile up at an alarming rate. And lying to her grandfather on Christmas Eve seemed worse than usual. But the die had been cast weeks ago. She had no choice except to say the things he expected to hear.

"We haven't found the perfect names, Grandpa. That's all."

"And what about you, Joe?" her grandfather asked. "Any favorites, yet?"

"Well, sir, the truth is, I've grown rather fond of Humphrey." Joe winked at Alicia.

Both his words and his teasing wink took her by surprise. She didn't know how to respond to either.

"Hmm." Grandpa Roger set his mug on the coffee table. "It's time to remind you that I won't be present when my great-grandchild is born. I'd like to make certain he or she isn't named in haste." He frowned at Joe. "Humphrey Palermo, indeed."

"I suppose you're right." Joe drew out his words, as if giving them serious consideration. "Actually, sir, I was thinking more along the lines of Teresa if it's a girl." He met Alicia's gaze. "After the baby's great-grandmother Harris."

Her eyes flooded with tears.

"That would have pleased my wife," Grandpa Roger said. "It pleases me, as well. Thank you from the bottom of an old man's heart." He paused, cleared his throat, then asked, "And if it's a boy?"

Even though she couldn't see him clearly, she knew Joe continued to watch her.

"The Palermos always give their firstborn sons the name Enrico, either as a first or middle name. It's a tradition I'd like to keep."

Determined not to burst into tears, she managed to say, "Your name isn't Enrico."

"I wasn't the first son. My older brother was still-born. He was named Enrico."

Did her grandfather wonder why she didn't know that?

Joe covered for her. "Guess I should have told you before now." He shrugged. "Losing him wasn't something my family talked about. I guess it became a habit not to."

She looked down at her belly. "We could call him Ricky."

"I like that." Joe took hold of her hand. "Ricky Palermo it is."

That was the moment when he should have told her he loved her. That was the moment when he should have told her he didn't want to be a husband for the holidays but for his entire life. He wanted her baby to be their baby. It didn't matter if the baby's first name was Ricky or Teresa or Humphrey as long as its last name was Palermo.

So why didn't he speak up on Christmas Eve? For the life of him he couldn't say. Call it nerves. Call it habit. Call it stupidity. Whatever the reason, he let that perfect moment pass.

Early on Christmas morning, Alicia made her way toward the kitchen. The warm aroma of coffee teased her nostrils, and she wondered how long Joe had been up.

When she saw him, leaning his backside against the counter, his legs angled before him, right ankle over left, she paused, wanting to enjoy the sight. He wore jeans and a sweatshirt. His feet were bare. In his right hand, he held a coffee mug, and he sipped from it, his eyes closed.

He looked…contented.

Oh, how she longed for that to be true. She loved him. She wanted him. She needed him. If only he could love, want and need her, too.

Was it possible? Could it happen?

As if she'd spoken aloud, he opened his eyes and

glanced her way. His smile was slow and sleepy. "Merry Christmas."

Her heart leaped in response. "Merry Christmas, Joe."

"Did you peek under the tree?"

"No."

"I'd've thought you the type to do that."

She returned his smile. "I am."

"Want some breakfast while we wait for Grandpa to wake up?"

She nodded.

"You set the table," he said, "and I'll scramble the eggs."

"Deal."

After setting down his coffee mug, he strode across the kitchen to the refrigerator. He was bent forward, looking inside the appliance, when Rosie jumped through the pet door, almost onto his foot. She slid to a halt, paws scrambling on the slick linoleum. Her back arched as high as it could go, and she hissed at him.

"Cat—" he pointed an index finger at the feline "—you and I are gonna come to terms before we're through."

Rosie growled but didn't move.

"Ask Rags. She'll tell you I'm one of the good guys."

Happiness flowed through Alicia as she watched and listened. If only they could stay like this forever.

Joe reached out, as if to pet the cat's head. Rosie

took a swipe at his hand, barely missing her target. Then she darted out of the kitchen.

He straightened and looked at Alicia. "I'm not crying uncle yet. I'm determined she'll get used to me."

I love you, Joe.

He stared at her, the look intense and unwavering; his smile faded.

Can you hear my heart?

"Alicia…"

Her pulse quickened.

"There's something I need to—" The sound of a closing door intruded on his words. He stopped and glanced toward the living room.

A few moments later Grandpa Roger appeared. "Merry Christmas."

"Merry Christmas, Grandpa."

"Merry Christmas, sir."

"Hope you haven't been waiting long."

"No, sir. We haven't."

Alicia wondered what Joe might have said if her grandfather had waited a little while longer.

Even though Grandpa Roger's arrival had been untimely, interrupting Joe's declaration of love, Joe wasn't discouraged. His heart told him he would find the right moment, an even better moment, to tell Alicia what he had to say. The future looked better than he'd imagined it could.

And this was the best of all Christmases, too.

When Joe was growing up, this time of the year had been about getting the latest gizmo. It had been about giving the gift with the most prestige or the biggest price tag.

But that wasn't what it was about in Alicia's home. It was about caring. He'd already witnessed that truth in the weeks he'd been here, but it became crystal clear when he opened Alicia's final gift to him.

In the box was a black leather day planner with his named etched on a gold plate in the lower right corner. The binder was nicer than the one he'd lost, but it was what he found inside the covers of the planner that truly touched his heart. Somehow, Alicia had duplicated most of the pages Rags destroyed, the ones Joe had given up for lost. Pages upon pages, including his extensive address book, were filled with her meticulous, legible handwriting.

"When did you find time to do this?"

"Here and there," she answered with a gentle smile.

Joe tried to think of something to say to express what he felt. Words eluded him. The best he could manage was a simple, "Thanks." He stood. "Now I've got something more for you. Sit tight."

He felt as excited as a kid in a candy store as he hurried out of the living room, into the kitchen and down the basement stairs. He knew Alicia would be surprised.

Satisfaction warmed Roger Harris.

If he'd had any doubts that Alicia and Joe belonged

together—which wasn't the case—those doubts would have been assuaged this morning. Watching the two of them was like looking into the face of love itself. Whatever problems had plagued them a couple of weeks earlier seemed to have been overcome.

Roger was thankful for that.

He stared at the Christmas tree with its dancing bubble lights, and his thoughts drifted back in time. He recalled the many Christmas mornings he and his beloved Teresa had shared. They'd had a good marriage, a blessed life. Of course, they'd had their share of heartaches and disappointments; no marriage ever escaped the bad times completely. The rain fell on the just and the unjust. But love had seen them through, seen them through and brought them closer together.

He lifted a silent prayer, asking God to grant many years, many *good* years, to his granddaughter and her husband. He prayed their love would sustain them no matter what tomorrow might bring.

Love always sustained.

Alicia shifted her position on the sofa, seeking a physical comfort that would not be found. The ache in her back had returned. If not for Joe and her grandfather, she'd have gone back to bed. But they would worry if she did, and the day was too perfect to allow that. Besides, she could hardly bear the suspense, waiting to see what had caused Joe to look so pleased with himself as he'd hurried from the room.

She heard him climbing the stairs and turned expectantly toward the kitchen doorway.

Before he came into view, he called out, "Close your eyes, Alicia."

"Joe—"

"Close 'em."

She released a dramatic sigh. "All right." She obeyed.

"Are they closed, sir?"

"They are, indeed," her grandfather replied.

Alicia folded her hands atop her abdomen, clenching them tightly while resisting the urge to peek. She heard Joe's footsteps on the hardwood floor, knew the moment he reached the sofa. She worried her lower lip between her teeth.

"Don't look yet."

She smiled. "You're enjoying this *way* too much, Joe Palermo."

"Uh-huh."

"Rat."

"Uh-huh."

She heard him set something on the floor.

"I got a call from Susie a while back."

"Susie?" Why was he talking about her assistant manager? And why would Susie call him?

"The supplier for that cradle you had your heart set on can't deliver one until spring."

Broadsided by the disappointing news, she forgot to keep her eyes closed. Her mouth was open to ask why he hadn't told her about the call—

And then she saw the wooden cradle. She looked from it to Joe and back again.

"I had it made," he said, answering her unspoken question. "I hope it's close enough to what you wanted."

"You had it made?" She slipped from the sofa and onto her knees, touching the smooth wood of the cradle.

"A local guy. He came highly recommended. A real artisan. I think he did a good job, even if he did have to work fast."

"It's beautiful. It's wonderful." She looked up. "How can I ever thank you for this?"

Joe knelt on the opposite side of the cradle. "You don't have to thank me."

He needed to be alone with her. He needed to tell her that he loved her and wanted to be her husband forever. He needed to tell her all the things he'd discovered since coming to stay with her. He'd waited long enough.

"Why don't we put this in the nursery now?"

She smiled. "Okay." Her response was tremulous, a telltale quiver in her lower lip that warned she was fighting tears.

Joe stood, then took both her hands in his and helped her do the same. He squeezed her fingers gently, reluctant to release his hold on her.

I'm not ever going to let go of you, Alicia.

He squeezed her fingers a second time, feeling

a bit misty-eyed himself. Then he reached for the cradle. "Lead the way."

She was almost to the hall when she stopped and looked back at him. "I've got a bumper and matching baby blanket down in the basement. I'm going to get them. I want to see how it all looks."

She hurried away before he could stop her.

He sighed. He supposed he could wait.

After all, what difference could a few minutes make in comparison to a lifetime?

Chapter Nineteen

Rags had been up to her old tricks again.

"What am I going to do with you?" Alicia muttered as she bent to retrieve the legal-size document with the canine teeth marks stamped upon it.

She was already walking toward Joe's office, meaning to leave the papers on his desk, when the words *Lease Agreement* penetrated her mind. She stopped still: her breath caught in her throat. With a heavy heart, she scanned the front page, then turned to the second.

Joseph Palermo was scrawled on the signature line. The contract was dated December 20.

Five days ago.

On Sunday he'd held her close and let her fall asleep in his arms.

On Monday he'd signed a lease for his new apartment.

She'd known all along he intended to move after

her grandfather returned to Arizona. This shouldn't have caught her by surprise, and yet it had. Because she'd started to believe he loved her.

But he didn't love her. He couldn't love her. He'd told her so several times, yet she'd chosen to ignore the truth. She couldn't do that any longer. She mustn't.

For his sake as well as for her own.

"Hey, you coming?" Joe called down to her.

"Yes." Still holding the lease agreement in one hand, she grabbed the bumper pad and blanket and cradle sheet, then walked toward the stairs. "I'm coming."

He waited for her in the kitchen. "I set the cradle near the window." He cupped her left elbow with one of his hands. "But I think I can feel a draft through the glass."

He was a good, kind man, she thought as she allowed him to propel her toward the nursery. He'd done her an enormous favor. It wasn't his fault he couldn't love her. She had no right to feel hurt and betrayed.

"So?" He released her arm and stepped ahead of her into the room. "What do you think?"

"I think we need to talk."

"No, I meant how does the cradle look in this room."

She dropped the items she carried. Everything except for the lease. That she held toward him. "Rags got into your office again."

He took the papers from her hand, his smile gone. "I didn't mean for you to see this."

"Why? Don't you want me to know where you live?"

"That isn't what I meant." He raked the fingers of one hand through his hair. "There's something I need to tell you. Something I should have said before now, only—"

Alicia turned toward the door. "Grandpa, could you come here please?"

"Alicia, wait. I need to—"

"Grandpa."

Her grandfather appeared in the doorway.

She reached out and took his hand. "Grandpa, we've been deceiving you, and it's time we put an end to it."

"Deceiving me?" He looked from Alicia to Joe and back again.

"Joe isn't the father of my baby. He…he agreed to stay with me and pretend to be my husband as a favor to me because I didn't want you to know the truth. I didn't want you to know I was pregnant and alone. I didn't want to worry you and put a strain on your heart."

"But you married Joe. I was there in the judge's chambers. Remember?"

"He's my husband in name only. We haven't… we haven't done anything we shouldn't. You should know that I was married to the baby's father. Briefly. He left me after three weeks. You were right about

not rushing into marriage. Grant didn't love me."
She lowered her gaze, not wanting to see the disappointment in her grandfather's eyes. "As soon as
you return to Arizona, the plan was for Joe to move
out. The marriage will be annulled. But I...I guess
there's no reason for him to wait to move, now that
you know."

"Alicia..." Joe began.

She turned around. "Don't. This isn't your fault.
It's all mine. The idea. The lies. Everything." Tears
filled her eyes. "It's time for you to go, Joe. It isn't
fair on either of us to drag it out. You've been a good
sport and a good friend. You've gone way beyond
what I should have asked of you. But the time of pretending is over."

"If you'd give me a chance—"

"Please don't argue. You know I'm right. Just pack
up and leave." With that she hurried out of the nursery, not wanting either of the men to see her as she
broke into a thousand pieces.

She went upstairs to one of the empty bedrooms
where she wouldn't have to see Joe remove his things
from her bedroom and the basement and the storage
room. It would hurt too much. She sat on the floor,
leaned her back against the wall and let the tears fall.

Her grandfather found her there some time later.

She looked up and asked, "Is Joe gone?"

"Not yet. He said he would return for the rest of
his things in a day or two." He pulled a folding chair
from where it leaned against the wall, opened it and

sat down beside her. "I'm going to remain in Idaho, if that's all right with you, Alicia."

Her throat grew tight with emotion. "You don't have to turn your life upside down for me. You love it in Arizona. All your friends are there."

"And all my family is here."

His words unleashed another wave of tears. He let her cry, her head now resting on his thigh, his hand stroking her hair. He didn't say another word. Simply waited and loved her in silence.

When the fresh storm of tears was spent, she told him everything. She didn't leave out a single detail. No excuses. No justification. Just the plain unvarnished truth. It was what she should have done from the outset.

"This is my fault, too," Grandpa Roger said when her story was complete.

"Yours?" She looked up.

He nodded. "I never should have pushed you and Joe into marriage. I should have trusted you more." He drew a breath and let it out on a sigh. "I was so sure that love would help you work things out in time. I see now that I was wrong."

"You weren't completely wrong, Grandpa. I love Joe."

His eyes widened. "Then why did you send him away?"

"Because he doesn't love me."

Joe put the last of his things in his SUV, then paused to look toward the house. Should he go inside and tell Alicia and her grandfather goodbye? No. She wanted him gone. She'd made it clear enough.

If she hadn't found that lease…

It was for the best, he supposed. He'd been about to declare his love for her. He would have if she'd let him. Maybe he'd been right all along. Maybe he would make a lousy husband and father. Maybe love wasn't enough in his case. Maybe God had stepped in to keep him from making a huge mistake.

He got into his vehicle, turned the key and backed out of the driveway.

It didn't take him long to drive to his Boise apartment. The streets were mostly deserted on Christmas Day. After all, people with families were with them.

Joe had no one.

The lease for his new residence had required the utilities be transferred to his name upon signing, so at least he wouldn't be without heat and lights until the next day. That was a blessing. He even had an activated phone jack. Of course, he didn't have a phone to plug into it, but he could pick one up tomorrow as soon as the stores opened. Until then, he had his cell phone.

Three trips between vehicle and apartment, and he'd moved in.

While the furnace pumped heat into the chilled rooms, Joe set his stereo to a station playing pop music—anything other than sounds of the holiday—then he flicked on the gas fireplace for ambience.

Neither served to improve his sense of isolation.

He thought of Alicia. He thought of the things he might have said, the things he might have done. He thought of what might have been.

But he didn't want to think. He didn't want to feel.

He got out his laptop, determined to work for the remainder of the day. He needed to start acting like the driven attorney he'd always been.

Alicia stood at the kitchen counter, holding the house key Joe had left behind, when her water broke. She gasped in surprise, uncertain at first what was happening. Then a band of pain tightened around her abdomen. It wasn't strong nor was it unbearable, but it was definitely pain.

"Grandpa, come quick!"

The key clattered to the floor as another rush of fluid was discharged.

"Grandpa!" she cried, gripping the counter with both hands.

"What is it?"

"My water broke." She looked at her grandfather as he entered the kitchen. "It's too soon. The baby isn't due for three weeks."

"Stay calm. Babies are known to set their own timetables." He patted her shoulder and gave her an encouraging smile, then he walked toward the telephone. "Where's your doctor's number?"

"On the bulletin board. Dr. Jamison." She pointed, grimacing as the pain strengthened. "In the upper right-hand corner. That's his business card."

"I'll call him. You go get your things together. We'll leave for the hospital as soon as we can get a cab."

The pain was lessening. "I could drive."

"Nonsense." Grandpa Roger lifted the receiver, then hesitated with his index finger poised above the keys. He glanced over his shoulder. "Go on. Get your suitcase."

As she headed toward her bedroom, she prayed silently for her baby to be all right.

Her small suitcase had been packed for a couple of weeks now. Actually, it had been packed and unpacked at least twice a week for the past two months. It sat on the floor right next to the door. She thought about opening it, maybe taking some things out, putting something else in. She was stopped by another pain spreading from the small of her back and wrapping around her belly.

"Please don't let anything go wrong," she whispered. She braced her abdomen between her hands. "We're going to be happy, you and I. I promise. I'll make you a good mother, Ricky."

Tears sprang to her eyes.

Humphrey, she reminded herself. Not Ricky Palermo. Humphrey Harris.

The pain receded once again. Alicia took a deep breath as she picked up her suitcase and started toward the kitchen. She stopped outside the nursery. Her gaze rested on the cradle. Inside it was the stuffed toy seal Joe had purchased at Bundles of Joy the day after he'd arrived in Idaho. She didn't know when he'd put it there. Probably while he was packing to leave.

She entered the nursery, crossed to the cradle and picked up the stuffed animal with her free hand. She pressed the toy to her chest, remembering the day Joe bought it. She wished...

But it was useless to wish for things she couldn't have.

She walked out of the nursery, still clutching the toy.

Despite all of Joe's best efforts, he accomplished nothing. His thoughts drifted again and again to Alicia. To Alicia and her grandfather and her baby. To the fact that he loved her and didn't want to lose her.

He'd made plenty of mistakes in the past month. It was his own fault she'd told him to leave. He should have told her he loved her the moment he'd realized it. But he didn't have to make the same mistake again. His heart told him that God wasn't trying to break them apart. Instead, God wanted to bring them together. He was sure of it. More sure than he'd been of anything in his life.

Joe's place was with Alicia, and somehow, some way, he was going to make her see that, too.

He grabbed his car keys and his coat and headed for the door.

Chapter Twenty

"It's too early," Alicia told the nurse. "I'm not due for three more weeks."

Nurse Beverly reassured her with a pat on the hand. "The fetal heartbeat is strong, and there are no signs of trouble. My guess is you've got a fully developed baby in there who's eager to meet the world."

"But—"

"Stop worrying, Ms. Harris. You're going to have enough to do in the next few hours."

"When will Dr. Jamison be in to see me?"

The nurse smiled patiently. "When he's finished his Christmas dinner, I imagine."

"He isn't on his way *now?*" Alicia's voice rose a notch with each word.

"You've got a ways to go, dear. Try to relax as much as you can. Take a walk around the halls. That sometimes speeds the process. And don't worry. The doctor will get here in plenty of time."

Alicia was positive Nurse Beverly chuckled as she left the birthing room.

A few minutes later Grandpa Roger appeared in the doorway. "Am I allowed in yet?"

"Yes. Come in."

"What news?" Her grandfather approached the bed.

"I'm supposed to relax and enjoy myself."

Grandpa Roger grinned.

She scooted off the table, feeling awkward, hating the hospital-issue gown. "If you laugh, Grandpa, I'll strangle you. I swear I will."

He nearly choked on it, but he managed to heed her warning.

"Come on. Let's walk." She put on her robe, then hooked her arm through his. Once they were out in the hall, she asked, "Did you call Susie?"

"Yes, but I got her answering machine."

"Feel up to being my coach?"

He patted her arm. "I'm honored to be asked." He chuckled softly. "Don't know how much help I'll be. In my day men were relegated to the waiting room."

She thought of Joe and the birthing classes. She remembered how she'd leaned against his chest, the way he'd touched her abdomen, the deep timbre of his voice.

I need you, Joe. I want you with me.

When nobody answered the door after several rings, Joe began to worry. Alicia's car was in the garage, but the house appeared to be empty. No sounds came from within. It was possible she'd seen who was outside and was ignoring him. If that was the case, he should leave.

But he couldn't shake the feeling something was wrong. He used the key Alicia kept hidden beneath a stone near the back porch.

"Alicia?"

He stepped into the kitchen.

"Mr. Harris?"

Rags galloped into the kitchen, acting delighted to see him.

"Hello, girl." He patted the dog's head. "Where's Alicia?"

The back of his neck tingled as he walked through the empty house, Rags following at his heels. He searched all the rooms on the main floor, then he checked the basement, then he checked the main floor a second time. He told himself not to panic, but it was getting harder to listen to the voice of reason.

Perhaps Alicia and Grandpa Roger were with a friend. Maybe they went with Susie to a movie. It hadn't exactly been a joyous Christmas Day in the Harris household. Maybe Alicia wanted to take her mind off him.

When he entered the master bedroom for the third time, he was greeted by Rosie's familiar growl. The feline was coiled on the sofa, watching him with a haughty glare.

"I don't have time to mess with you, cat."

He turned to leave and then stopped.

The suitcase. Alicia's maternity suitcase. She'd kept it by the door, and now it was gone.

His pulse quickened with alarm. The "don't panic" command was useless now. He raced to the kitchen where he yanked the phone directory from its drawer. With clumsy fingers he leafed through the pages until he found the listing for the hospital. In the midst of dialing the number, he had to hang up twice due to punching the wrong keys. But finally he did it right.

He barely let the receptionist say the hospital's name before he asked. "Has an Alicia Harris checked into the maternity ward?"

He assumed the following silence meant the woman was checking her records.

"Yes, sir. She's there now."

"Thanks," he said a split second before dropping the receiver in its cradle.

He was out the door in a flash.

Mothers in labor walked the halls of the maternity ward, going around and around and around the same circuitous route. Occasionally one of them would change directions to break the monotony. When they passed one another, they smiled, as if their conditions had made them friends, comrades in arms.

Alicia's pains had grown in intensity, and still the nurse said she had a long way to go before serious labor would begin. Little Humphrey Harris, Alicia decided around her third hour of labor, was going to be an only child.

At five o'clock, she insisted Grandpa Roger go to the cafeteria for supper.

When he tried to argue with her, she snapped, "You'll do me no good if you make yourself sick. Now please go and eat something."

She was ashamed of her tone, but there was no taking the words back.

After her grandfather left the room, Alicia sat on the window ledge and stared at the darkening sky.

I wonder how close I am to Joe's apartment.

She'd recognized the address on the lease. She knew the upscale complex was near the Boise River. If the hospital had more floors... If the ancient oaks and elms didn't rise so tall above the stately homes... If—

"But she's my wife!"

Alicia turned as the door to her room burst open and Joe pushed his way past the nurse.

"I'm sorry, Ms. Harris," the flustered young woman said. "I'll call security."

She rose to her feet, pulling her robe more closely around her. "No. It's all right."

The nurse didn't look convinced.

Joe took another step into the room. "Tell her I'm your husband."

"We're married." That was somehow more honest than what he'd asked her to say.

"I came as soon as I found out," he said.

"How did you know?"

He glanced at the nurse, his gaze demanding she leave them alone.

"It's all right," Alicia said again. "Really."

Joe waited until the door swung closed before saying, "I went back to the house. It was empty. Your suitcase was gone."

"Oh."

"Do you want to know why?"

"Why what?"

"Why I went back to the house."

She crossed her arms over her chest. "I assume you left something behind."

"Yes. As a matter of fact, I did." He took another step forward. "You."

"Oh, Joe." She turned toward the window, watching as the city came alive with lights. "You don't have to pretend any longer."

"I'm not pretending. This is for real. This is the most real I've been in my life. I love you, Alicia."

Another pain crept around her abdomen, making it difficult to think, difficult to breathe. She did her best not to let on.

"I want to be your husband in every definition of the word."

Sheer resolve kept her voice steady. "You don't want kids, and in case you haven't noticed…I do. And very soon, too."

"I was wrong."

"Were you?" She faced him again. "I think you

stated your feelings quite clearly in your daddy clause."

He frowned. "My daddy clause?"

"In the prenuptial." She was *not* going to cry. She was *not* going to cry. "About my baby."

"Oh. That."

The urge to cry vanished, driven away by anger. "Yes, *that! This* is the baby you didn't want." She pressed her hands against the sides of her abdomen. "*This* is the baby you wanted to make certain no one thought was yours. *This* was—"

Her words were cut short by a sharp, searing pain. She gasped, and her knees buckled. Joe caught her in his arms before she could fall.

"What is it?"

"I think it's time," she managed to say through gritted teeth. "Help me to the bed and then call the nurse."

Things happened quickly after that.

The attractive birthing room with its soft lights, muted wallpaper and homey furnishings changed in an instant to the epitome of modern medical technology. Bright overhead lights swung out of a closet, slipping into position above the bed. All the necessary hospital equipment and paraphernalia appeared from different nooks and cubbyholes, as if by magic. Nurses bustled about doing nurse-type things.

Joe was in the way. He figured most men were at a time like this. As a matter of fact, he would have liked to be anywhere else in the world rather than here. He felt useless, and that wasn't a feeling he was used to or comfortable with.

But it would take more than discomfort to drive him out now.

He stepped to the side of Alicia's bed. "I'll write you a new daddy clause."

She gave him a sharp look.

"Every firstborn Palermo male is named Enrico. We need to get that settled before he gets here."

She clenched her jaw, and a groan came up from deep in her chest.

Joe looked at a nurse. "Is she all right?"

"She's about to have a baby."

"Where can I get pen and paper?"

"Try the desk," the nurse answered. He was walking toward the door when he heard her add, "Men. Anything to keep them out of the way."

"I'll be right back, Alicia."

He yanked open the door...and there stood Roger Harris. The older man didn't seem surprised to see him.

"Evening, sir."

"Evening, Joe."

"Will you marry us before our baby arrives?"

Alicia's grandfather raised an eyebrow. "You are married."

"Just legally, sir. This would be different. I love her. I want to promise to love and cherish her before God."

Grandpa Roger smiled. "I'll do it if that's what Alicia wants."

"She's going to want it." He took off down the hall toward the nurses' station.

Breathing hard from the most recent contraction, Alicia asked the nurse. "Where's the doctor?"

"He's on his way. He'll be here soon."

The door opened. Alicia thought it would be the doctor. It wasn't.

Joe strode across the spacious room, legal pad in hand. Alicia's grandfather was right behind him.

She leaned back on the pillow. "I don't think you should be in here."

"I'm your birth coach. Remember? I *do* belong here." He held out the paper, covered with his bold penmanship. "Read this."

"Are you crazy?" She sounded as irritable as she felt. "In case you can't tell, I'm *busy*."

He grinned.

She considered homicide.

"Okay, I'll do it." He leaned close, and in a soft voice began to read. "I, Joseph Palermo, do solemnly swear that I will love, cherish and honor my wife, Alicia Harris Palermo, for the rest of my life."

The bright overhead lights seemed to recede. All she could see was Joe. All she could hear was his beloved voice.

"I will be faithful and true and will never hurt her intentionally. I will provide for her welfare and support her pursuit of her own dreams, whatever they may be. I further declare that I will be a loving father to our child, born this Christmas Day, and I will raise him or her, in partnership with my wife, to the best of my abilities. Should God bless us with more children in the years to come, I will do the same for them."

Alicia wondered if this was the strangest delivery room scene these nurses had ever witnessed.

"And finally, should there be any question, I promise to love the dogs who chew up my important papers and the cats who take chunks out of my hide. I'll love them because they are hers."

She couldn't see him any longer. Her eyes were swimming in tears. And if she wasn't mistaken, at least one of the nurses was sniffling.

Joe took her hand. "I love you. I don't want to be your holiday husband. I want to be your husband for a lifetime. Humphrey is our own bundle of joy. You know it as much as I do. I want your grandfather to marry us again. For real this time. Let me chop down all your Christmas trees. Let me drink your spiced cider while we watch the bubble lights bubble. Marry me, Alicia. Say yes."

She would have answered, if not for the contraction that gripped her. She groaned and gritted her teeth.

"I think that's a yes, sir. Time to say the appropriate words. And I think you'd better hurry, too."

Epilogue

New Year's Day

Alicia knew Joe had been watching her sleep. She'd discovered him doing so every morning since her return from the hospital.

"Morning, sleepyhead," he whispered near her ear.

She rolled onto her side, bringing their foreheads close together, and looked at him. The light from the lamp on the nightstand allowed her to see the loving expression in his eyes, an expression that made her feel all warm and tingly on the inside.

"Good morning," she responded softly.

He kissed her, one of those sweet, slow kisses that made her feel cherished, the kind she could never get enough of. "Happy New Year."

Ricky stirred in his cradle. A whimper soon followed.

"Little tyrant." Joe kissed her again. "Stay here. I'll get him."

It was one of those simple things in her life that Alicia took great pleasure in, watching him be the daddy he hadn't thought he wanted to be.

Clad in the shorts and T-shirt he wore for pajamas, Joe rose and walked to the cradle. He leaned over the baby's bed, speaking softly in words Alicia couldn't quite make out. In short order he changed Ricky's diaper, as if he'd done it a thousand times.

Cat's paws made pattering sounds across the floor, announcing Rosie's arrival. A moment later, she began to purr.

"Not now, Rosie," Joe said.

Although Alicia couldn't see it, she knew the cat was winding her way around Joe's ankles, her tail carried high as she demanded Joe's affections. The change in the feline's attitude toward her husband was just one more in a long list of small miracles that had followed Ricky's arrival.

Joe lifted their son from the cradle and returned to the bed where he lay on his back, holding the baby on his chest. Ricky fussed a moment or two longer, then fell back to sleep.

"Guess he wasn't ready for breakfast yet." He held out his free arm. "Come here and join us."

Alicia was only too happy to oblige. She slid across the mattress, drawing close against his side, her cheek resting on his shoulder.

"Better sleep while you can."

"I know."

But she didn't close her eyes right away. She took pleasure in watching them, father and son, Joe and Ricky Palermo, the ski bum and his little mogul monster. She smiled, remembering when she'd overheard Joe refer to himself and the baby by those nicknames. He'd been carrying Ricky through a new layer of snow on the sidewalks on the day he brought his family home from the hospital.

His family. Were any two words more wonderful than those?

She closed her eyes, saying a silent prayer of thanks to God for the joy He'd allowed to flow into and over her life. Despite the many mistakes she'd made, despite all the ways she'd gone wrong, despite all of her sins—both large and small—He had blessed her, blessing upon blessing upon blessing.

"What are you smiling about?" Joe whispered.

"Everything," she answered without opening her eyes a second time. "I'm smiling about everything."

* * * * *

Dear Reader

I love the Christmas season. I also love babies, and God has blessed me with two wonderful daughters and six beautiful grandchildren, all of whom have grown up much too fast. I suppose it isn't necessary to also mention that I'm a romantic. So blending romance and Christmas and the promise of a new life in *Bundle of Joy* was particularly fun. I hope reading Alicia and Joe's story has lifted your spirits and given you pleasure.

Alicia and Joe first "introduced" themselves to me in 1998, and I was quickly enchanted by the possibilities for their love story. Now, years later, I'm delighted that Love Inspired is bringing their story to life again in *Bundle of Joy*.

I invite you to visit my website at www.robinleehatcher.com to keep up on the latest releases as well as to learn about my backlist.

In the grip of His grace,

Robin Lee Hatcher

Questions for Discussion

1. Alicia decides a ruse is the simplest solution to her problems. Do you agree with her approach? Why or why not? What advice would you have given to someone in her situation?

2. What parallels exist between Alicia's situation and that of an expectant young mother in Jerusalem more than two thousand years ago?

3. Though Joe's path to fatherhood is an unusual one, he embraces it by the end of the story. What happened during the course of the story to convince him of the benefits of fatherhood?

4. Alicia and Joe's friendship rekindled when they found each other online. How has the use of the internet helped your friendships? How has it harmed them?

5. Alicia reveals her feelings to Joe before she is sure how he feels about her. Was that a brave step? Would you have made a similar one? Why or why not?

6. Grandpa Roger expresses strong feelings about the importance of matrimony and he's fortunate that he can influence Alicia and Joe, though not

in the way he expected. How can you influence young people around you with the same message?

7. Joe prays: "Lord, she acted out of love for him. Was it so wrong?" What would you say to him? How is his prayer answered in the story?

8. What information do Grandpa Roger's stories about his life with his wife, Teresa, give to Joe and Alicia? How are they helped by his insights?

9. How does the Christmas setting make its appearance in the story? What traditions do Alicia and her grandfather share?

10. How does Alicia's pregnancy affect her decision-making? In what way does it help? In what way does it pose problems?

11. Joe's Christmas treat was a nice surprise for Alicia. What pleasant surprises have you received over the Christmas holidays? Share a story with the group.

12. What blessings have your children brought to you? How has Alicia been a blessing to her grandfather?

REQUEST YOUR FREE BOOKS!

2 FREE RIVETING INSPIRATIONAL NOVELS
PLUS 2 FREE MYSTERY GIFTS

YES! Please send me 2 FREE Love Inspired® Suspense novels and my 2 FREE mystery gifts (gifts are worth about $10). After receiving them, if I don't wish to receive any more books, I can return the shipping statement marked "cancel." If I don't cancel, I will receive 4 brand-new novels every month and be billed just $4.74 per book in the U.S. or $5.24 per book in Canada. That's a savings of at least 21% off the cover price. It's quite a bargain! Shipping and handling is just 50¢ per book in the U.S. and 75¢ per book in Canada.* I understand that accepting the 2 free books and gifts places me under no obligation to buy anything. I can always return a shipment and cancel at any time. Even if I never buy another book, the two free books and gifts are mine to keep forever.

123/323 IDN F5AN

Name	(PLEASE PRINT)

Address	Apt. #

City	State/Prov.	Zip/Postal Code

Signature (if under 18, a parent or guardian must sign)

Mail to the Harlequin® Reader Service:
IN U.S.A.: P.O. Box 1867, Buffalo, NY 14240-1867
IN CANADA: P.O. Box 609, Fort Erie, Ontario L2A 5X3

**Are you a current subscriber to Love Inspired Suspense books and want to receive the larger-print edition?
Call 1-800-873-8635 or visit www.ReaderService.com.**

* Terms and prices subject to change without notice. Prices do not include applicable taxes. Sales tax applicable in N.Y. Canadian residents will be charged applicable taxes. Offer not valid in Quebec. This offer is limited to one order per household. Not valid for current subscribers to Love Inspired Suspense books. All orders subject to credit approval. Credit or debit balances in a customer's account(s) may be offset by any other outstanding balance owed by or to the customer. Please allow 4 to 6 weeks for delivery. Offer available while quantities last.

Your Privacy—The Harlequin® Reader Service is committed to protecting your privacy. Our Privacy Policy is available online at www.ReaderService.com or upon request from the Harlequin Reader Service.
We make a portion of our mailing list available to reputable third parties that offer products we believe may interest you. If you prefer that we not exchange your name with third parties, or if you wish to clarify or modify your communication preferences, please visit us at www.ReaderService.com/consumerchoice or write to us at Harlequin Reader Service Preference Service, P.O. Box 9062, Buffalo, NY 14269. Include your complete name and address.

LISDIR13R

REQUEST YOUR FREE BOOKS!
2 FREE WHOLESOME ROMANCE NOVELS IN LARGER PRINT
PLUS 2
FREE
MYSTERY GIFTS

❊❊❊❊❊❊❊❊❊❊❊❊❊❊❊❊❊❊❊❊❊

HEARTWARMING™

❊❊❊❊❊❊❊❊❊❊❊❊❊❊❊❊❊❊❊❊❊

Wholesome, tender romances

HWDIR13R

ReaderService.com

Manage your account online!

- Review your order history
- Manage your payments
- Update your address

---

*We've designed
the Harlequin® Reader Service
website just for you.*

Enjoy all the features!

- Reader excerpts from any series
- Respond to mailings and
  special monthly offers
- Discover new series available to you
- Browse the Bonus Bucks catalog
- Share your feedback

Visit us at:
ReaderService.com

RS13